THE BUREAU OF THEM

A SNOWBOOKS HORROR NOVELLA

Proudly published by Snowbooks

Snowbooks Ltd.
email: info@snowbooks.com
www.snowbooks.com.

British Library Cataloguing in Publication Data.
A catalogue record for this book is available
from the British Library.

Paperback: 978-1-911390-95-4
Ebook: 978-1-911390-96-1

THE BUREAU OF THEM

CATE GARDNER

THE BUREAU OF THEM

ONE

The man at the abandoned office building's window would be a collection of shadow and dust. It wouldn't be Glynn. Katy brushed her fringe away from her eyes. Glynn was dead. The dust-built figure's fingertips touched the glass. Katy blinked back tears, determined not to look away. To have Glynn back for just a moment was better than never at all.

"Katy," Nathan said, "you still with us?"

Katy wanted to ask the same question of the dust boy. If only breath would mist his side of the glass. It didn't. It couldn't.

"I said, are you still with us?"

Nathan's words should be inconsequential. Instead, for Katy, they sent memories swirling. She could feel Glynn's hand in hers, his breath on her face, the vibration of his lips against her ear. No one ever noticed the wreck their words made of her . She should be over it now, they'd say. Hasn't Glynn been dead for a year?

Thirteen months, twelve days, seven hours, some minutes.

If she could reassemble Glynn from shadow and dust, she would. If she could remove this window without disturbing the illusion, she would, although it wouldn't be of any more use than a collection of old photographs and warped memories. It wasn't Glynn. It couldn't be him. The ghost traced a heart in the dust. Her knees sagged.

"What's so interesting about that building?" Nathan asked.

She couldn't tell him. No more than she could look away. If she turned for just a second the illusion would dismantle and she'd never win Glynn back.

"We're going to the pub on Friday. The Old School. Steph said they're fighting to keep it open and they might succeed if the old gang met up there. We used to drink that place dry. Glynn..."

Sometimes other people forgot Glynn was dead too.

"Crap! Is that the time? I have to head back to work but," he said, turning her to face him, "are you okay? I'm worried about you. We're all worried about you."

She wanted to ask Nathan if he could see Glynn, but she daren't. Instead, she replied, "Fine. Just a little distracted. Sorry."

"Daniel will be there on Friday."

"I'm not interested."

Her friends were determined to set her up with Daniel, a slick boy in a pressed suit who would never be her type. Had they forgotten Glynn's laughing eyes, his dishevelled hair, and easy smile? If Daniel died, he'd look back at her from polished chrome.

"Friday then," Nathan said.

Katy nodded. With a wave, Nathan turned and ran across the road, taking no heed of the traffic despite the fact they'd both lost someone they loved there. No wonder she saw Glynn here. Witnesses claimed Glynn strolled out into the traffic as if the road were empty, walking into the path of a coach. Dead at the scene. Although she hadn't been there, the screech of metal and crunch of bone beneath tyres woke her most mornings. She turned back to the window and its dust ghost. In the building's doorway, a tramp coughed into his fist, a guttural sound, thick with phlegm. She hadn't noticed him there before. The tramp rattled his box of trinkets. Katy ignored him and approached the window where the dust boy continued to watch.

"It's not you," she said.

"You're not the first to talk to your dead here," the tramp said.

"Glynn's not here," she said, not questioning how he knew she was talking to a ghost.

"If you say so."

The mind played awful tricks and it wasn't as if this was the first time she'd seen Glynn since he'd died, it was just that he usually dissipated within seconds or proved to be a stranger with a similar look. Behind the window, the accumulation of dust and shadows stepped back. Boys formed from inanimate things couldn't move. The window emptied. Katy rushed to the doorway and drummed her fists against wood and glass. The tramp continued to shake the collection of trinkets in his cardboard box.

The door rattled against its frame but didn't open. With a final thump, Katy considered there might be something within the tramp's box she could use to jimmy the door open.

The tramp held a key in the curve of his palm. When Katy bent to grab it, his fingers snapped over the key and he rubbed the fingers of his other hand together. Katy dug into her purse and removed a five-pound note. She wedged the note beneath a plastic cube and a metallic owl in the tramp's box. He gave her the key.

It fitted the lock.

The lock unfastened with a click. Katy's hand rested against the door, but she didn't push it open. The tramp didn't urge her either way. She could open it a little, call into the dark and see if anyone answered. If Glynn were in there, he wouldn't ignore her. Of course, he couldn't be in there because Glynn was dead. The door shuddered beneath her hand. Shapes moved behind wired glass, indistinct against layers of dirt. Beside her, the tramp gathered his box and clutched it to his chest. Spit dribbled into his beard.

If he had the key, he must have been inside and if he'd been inside it was possible other vagrants lived within the building. She'd seen a man, a stranger. She hadn't seen Glynn. Of course, if she didn't push the door open and see whoever it was that almost resembled her Glynn then Glynn would never let her go.

She didn't want him to let her go. She didn't want to let go.

"Who's in there?" she asked both the tramp and whoever was behind the door.

Now was the time to run. She didn't move, frozen in place by hope, by want, by a key that opened a long-abandoned door. Looking at the key, she saw it wasn't the type of key to open an office building. Its ironwork was intricate and ornate, its length long and Victorian, whereas the building was 1960s at the earliest. Behind the door, shadows swelled in number. Bellies pressed against glass, shirt buttons straining, waiting for her to open the door. Why didn't they open it themselves?

"Are you certain you want to see him again?"

It wouldn't be Glynn. The tramp grabbed her arm. She pulled away from him, batting him off. Tears ran down her cheek. If she thought Glynn was inside the building, really thought it, then of course she would want to see him again, but it wasn't Glynn, it was a tramp. All the same, she nodded in answer to the tramp's question. He grabbed her arm again and this time pulled her to the side of the building.

The door opened. It seemed she'd formed a plug, keeping those within the building trapped, for when she stepped onto the pavement the wind stilled and people began to file through the open doorway. They didn't look like tramps — too ordered, too co-ordinated, too ghastly. Each of them wore either a grey dress or a

4

grey suit, their pallor the same washed-out shade; easy to believe they were dead.

A laugh trembled up her throat. Snot joined the tears rolling down her face. She wiped away both. This was a nightmare. About her the dead swarmed, although swarm didn't seem the correct term for their orchestrated movements. About them, about her, the world continued as normal, undisturbed by this gathering of ghosts. She shivered against the building, rough concrete digging into her back. She shook her head as if to prove to the world she thought them an illusion.

"They're not ghosts."

The tramp neither confirmed nor denied her statement.

The tide of ghosts parted to reveal Glynn amongst them. Her hand reached out but touched only air and perhaps the edge of a cotton jacket coated in grey dust. They moved away from her. Ripples, distortions cast by sharp sunlight. Sobs shuddered through her. She'd lost her mind.

"You left me."

The dead turned on their heels, sweeping grey dust arcs against the pavement. Closing rank about Glynn, they flowed along The Strand.

"No."

For a moment, the tramp, the wind or perhaps a ghost (ridiculous!) held her against the building. Then she fell forward, dropping to her knees. She scrambled to her feet and chased after the dead but they were too fast. Even at a run, she couldn't match their magnificent strides.

"Glynn."

They didn't turn at her cry. Grey against grey, they'd moved so far that she could no longer pick Glynn out from the sombre crowd. At the corner of James Street, the wind pushed Katy back; it stole her breath and battered her thighs and chest with distinct punches. When at last she turned the corner, Katy caught a glimpse of the tail end of the group before they faded against the reality of people, bus shelters and pubs. The dead erased from the landscape as if they'd never existed.

"Glynn," she said, more of a whisper now, pain cutting across her belly, folding her in two.

Thirteen months dropped to a single minute. Katy wiped the heel of her palm beneath her eyes, smearing the building's dust and dirt across her cheek. The veins in her forehead throbbed, pulsing toward headache and only when a bus driver sounded his horn did she realise she'd wandered into the road. She stepped onto the pavement, dazed and disorientated. She'd thought she understood the full weight of grief but all that had passed before was a mere pinprick compared to this weight that threatened to fell her. It had almost been easier to think she would never see him again. Hope ached more than no hope.

Yes, easier to think he'd gone forever.

She looked up the curve of James Street desperate for the dead to become visible again even if they surrounded and threatened her. The air felt empty, stealing her breath. Empty because she had swallowed the world, and all its pain now rested within her desperate to break through her fragile skin. It hurt to breathe. It hurt to exist. Steadying herself against the wall, Katy turned back onto The Strand. Again, the tramp sat within the doorway of the abandoned building (or rather not so abandoned), his polished shoes poking from the entranceway, a box of trinkets positioned between his knees. He'd known what would happen. She was certain of that. He'd expected the dead to rush from the building.

"Who were they?" she asked, her voice trembling. "Was it him? Was it my Glynn?"

The tramp's fingerless gloves snagged on the sharpened edge of a key while the other contents of the box rolled to a far corner. Metallic owl, coloured blocks, cocktail umbrella and other assorted crap. Katy stole the key from his box. This time it didn't fit the lock, its ornate edge too large for the Yale keyhole.

"It is of no use to you now," the tramp said. "You get to open the door once. Now you'll have to wait for them to return and open the door for you. That's how it is with the dead."

He spoke of them as if they were real and not a figment of her grief.

"Locks and keys take time to wear apart."

The wind pushed her against the door, eager to press her into the building. Her hair whipped about her face, concealing her red-rimmed eyes and nose. The far-too-large key scraped against the outer edges of the lock. Frustrated, Katy slammed her knee against the door.

"Open, damn it!"

Perhaps she should try sesame, abracadabra, or some other magic word. I love you. A sob broke. She broke. The world couldn't offer her a glimpse of Glynn and then steal him back. She tapped her forehead against the door and didn't care about the dirt, what passers-by may think. He'd been here, within reach of her hand, and now, he was gone again. She turned and looked across the road to the approximate spot where Glynn had died. A man in a dark grey suit watched her from the central reservation. She'd have thought nothing of him only he slowly faded from view until only an outline of him remained.

"Did you see...?" she turned to ask the tramp, but he too had vanished.

She stepped away from the building, wrapped her jacket tight about her body and walked ghost-like through the weave of traffic both human and vehicular.

TWO

The woman tethered to the desk by cobwebs stared at the door and the echo of a living woman pressed into its glass. Death froze the cobwebbed woman, left her petrified. If she were a ghost, why didn't she fade? If she were a zombie, why didn't she crave brains? If she was still in the world, why couldn't she step into the sunlight and breathe?

Sometimes the woman recalled her name was Isobel and that she'd been in love with a man named Peter. Sometimes she saw Peter standing at her reception desk, chattering away as if the gulf of life and death wasn't standing between them. He saw only the wood of this desk, whereas Isobel felt the weight of dirt.

Mostly she wondered why the living chased after the dead when the dead wanted no part of them.

"Shoo," she whispered, disturbing neither cobweb nor dust.

The living woman moved from the door. A coincidence.

The living never heard her and neither did the dead.

THREE

Katy saw no more ghosts on the way home. She got off the bus and waited for a moment in the bus shelter, catching her breath, trying and failing to make sense of what she'd seen. Shattered Perspex crunched beneath her shoes. She'd read in the local paper that the council were considering removing all bus shelters due to the cost of continuous repair. Every night gangs stole into her world leaving a trail of destruction and scrawled graffiti as if they needed to assert their place. Dust tickled the inside of her nostrils — not surprising considering the dirt that had covered the window of the office building and how she'd all but snorted the dust in her attempt to enter. She sneezed.

As she reached into her pocket for a tissue, something fell out and rebounded against broken slices of Perspex. The metallic owl from the tramp's box rolled to the pavement edge. Katy picked it up. She turned it over in her hand as though doing so would explain how she'd come to own it. A curious little thing, jointed wings vibrating in the breeze. She'd give it back tomorrow. Now she had a reason to return to the building.

Glynn wouldn't be there. She had to remember that.

Katy dropped the owl into her pocket and crossed the road. Traffic was thin as she headed towards the children's playground and into the car park which surrounded the tower blocks, which were known locally as The Flats. With The Flats due for demolition and most of the residents having already moved out, the weave of buildings formed a ghost town. She peered up the long stretch of the nearest block. Graffiti tags decorated concrete, red paint running down the block; to look like blood she supposed (as if the area was bleeding), with a devil-like man melting within said blood. By her rough calculations, and despite the impossibility of it, the artist had left their mark between the thirteenth and fourteenth floors. The shade of red, the painful drip of paint, reminded Katy of Glynn's artwork. The small devil-like man made her think of Glynn's bus sketches (as she liked to call them). He'd sketch a passenger's image and dissatisfied with his attempt, he'd crumple the paper and litter the bus with it. Sometimes, Katy thought Glynn's subjects creased and folded beneath the weight of his fingers as if they knew he was dissatisfied with their image.

She'd worried he'd grow tired of her face. She'd worried about so much, silly things, when instead she should have concentrated on wrapping her arms around him, of kissing him, of cherishing every smile. She missed his smile. Her chest pained. She hadn't felt this degree of grief in months and now she was back to day one and the words, 'Glynn is dead'. Glynn is dead.

Distracted by the art, Katy's hip slammed into a supermarket trolley, which rolled back and forth in the car park as though searching for something lost. Its wheels screeched against concrete. The twenty-three stories of each of The Flats cast long shadows, ghosts stretching across tarmac. Their shadows ended at a broken fruit machine someone had abandoned in a parking space.

On Boaler Street, the metal boards covering the doors of the old cinema creaked back. They bent at an unnatural angle as if wanting to rip free of the cinema and reveal the ruin inside.

The Cosy Cinema had closed in the late 1960s, the spectral sign above its door all that remained to indicate the building's original purpose. Weeds sprouted from the its roof, from the cracks in its walls, trailed down red-black bricks. In the distance, a car engine backfired and its sudden noise caused Katy to note that the streets were empty and silent. There were no other pedestrians, no traffic, not even a pigeon to coo against the anomaly, as if she were alone in the world. Metal creaking broke the silence as things smashed within the cinema; sounded as if the upper balcony had crashed into the auditorium. Brick dust puffed from the open doorway. Spooked, Katy hurried on.

Too many ghosts this day.

Back home, she stood in the vestibule with her back to the front door, hand clasping the stolen owl, her breath the only sound. She ached to hear movement within the house, for Glynn to call out to her. She hated the silent rooms. Dropping her keys beside the phone, Katy picked up a doodle Glynn had sketched onto the phone pad — a heart erupting from a tiny man. He loves you. She traced the outline of the heart. If she crumpled the doodle in her fist, would someone somewhere fold in on himself? She'd often thought there was magic within Glynn's drawings, that he owned a piece of those he drew. He'd drawn her so many times, too many times, thrown sketches of her in the bin and torn her face in half. Only when things were bad and mostly they were good. She'd never crumpled beneath the weight of his fingers. She'd always smoothed out his frustrations. A knock at the front door startled her.

Spooked, Katy pressed her hand to her chest, caught her breath and opened the front door. There was no one there. She stepped into the street and found it empty. Perhaps her neighbour, Mrs Jenkins, had seen her rush home and worried something was wrong; most people worried about her these days. Katy closed the door, fingers resting a moment on wood ready to open it if someone knocked again. When no one did, she turned back to the telephone and phoned her friend, Steph.

"Do you think we ever truly end?" Katy asked.

"Glynn's dead, Katy."

"Oh, I know. It's just sometimes I think I see ghosts."

Steph sighed. Steph had done a lot of sighing in the last thirteen months as if Katy's grief was a weight on her chest. Katy dug into her pocket and curled her fingers around the metallic owl. Perhaps some people were so full of life they found a way to come back, forming a new life however thin the fabric of it. Boys with a ready smile and quick wit didn't rot to nothing.

"What if he didn't die?"

Of course, she knew he had. Even if she had seen Glynn earlier, however preposterous the thought, he had been a ghost and not a living man. She'd stood over his coffin, had touched his frozen skin.

"It wasn't him, Kate. You didn't see him."

The metallic owl flapped its wings within Katy's fist. She pulled it from her pocket. The owl danced on her palm proving life could exist in unexpected places.

"It wasn't him," Steph repeated.

Glynn had filled every room he entered. You'd hear his laugh before he arrived. People like Glynn didn't just stop. Again, someone knocked at the door and this time the letterbox flapped up. Katy stooped to glare at the snooper but there appeared to be no one there. The letterbox held up by the wind or its own will.

"Katy, it wasn't him."

Third time's a charm.

"I know," Katy said, a sob punctuating her words.

FOUR

From his perch on the roof of the forgotten cinema, Yarker Ryland peered at the girl who weaved between the ghosts of The Flats. When she approached the cinema, he swooped, dropping onto the metal grating that covered the door and bounced on it to catch her attention. She jerked at the sound but he didn't feel like a jerk for scaring her. It was his role in...death, he supposed. Inside the cinema the dead screeched, hollered, and tore apart chairs and dusty concession stands as if doing so would tear away the fabric of their remembered lives. It pained to have the weight of life surround you. They deserved to destroy things.

The girl rushed on, slipped around a corner and thought she hid from them but they had her interest now. Once seen you had to chase after your dead.

He'd chased after his dead until he'd found his death on the roof of an abandoned office building. The living don't realise that the dead don't give a shit about the living. Why should they? Why should he? His belly was hollow with the want for food and a good half-pint of beer. Did that girl care he couldn't have those things? Of course she didn't. You're dead, she'd say, and food is for the living.

"We still count," Yarker said. His voice carried only as stink in the wind. Like bad eggs, he'd heard a man once say when Yarker had screamed into his face. "We will not be forgotten."

Why did the living think it was okay to forget the dead? Persuading those in mourning to look to the future and erase the past, as if the dead were chalk on a blackboard that a quick swipe with a duster could obliterate. Yarker bounced several times on the metal grating until it thwacked up and launched him into the dark of the cinema. He fell onto his back, looking at the ceiling where spiders busied themselves constructing webs on top of webs undisturbed by the cinema's ghostly patrons. He wondered if there were spider ghosts who systematically trawled dark corners to destroy forgotten webs. He'd once eaten a web when walking to work. It had stretched from hedge to lamppost and he'd walked straight through it with his stupid mouth open. He'd eat a web now if he could. He'd eat anything to stave off this hunger. Offering the cinema a plaster-shattering moan, Yarker jumped up.

He wished he'd chased after the girl and swirled around her with his arms flapping; he wished he'd made her see him. Instead, he danced about Peter, the man who walked with the dead. Peter balanced on a cinema seat, flinching whenever debris flew too close to his breakable head. However, for Yarker, rushing in circles about Peter didn't have the same effect as it would over someone who couldn't see him. Peter looked bored and tired, perhaps hungry. He'd watched Peter steal scraps from kitchen cupboards and litter bins, holding his mouth under a running tap to wet his parched throat. Yarker raced across the cinema. Hurtling over broken chairs and fallen masonry, he launched himself at the wall, jumping up and grabbing a fist full of spider web and spider. He raced back to Peter and began to swirl bits of web about the boy.

Peter looked as petrified as his cobwebbed girlfriend who sat in reception back at the office.

"You can't escape," Yarker said, and Peter neither agreed nor disagreed with the statement. "You belong to us. You may as well be dead."

Peter balled his hands and drummed them against his thighs. The anger within him could bring down the world whether he was dead or not.

Yarker pressed his lips to Peter's ear and said, "We will break you." Yarker skipped up the stairs to the stage, posed in front of the cinema screen and shouted, "I'm ready for my close-up, Mr Kubrick."

FIVE

Katy woke to the feel of Glynn's arms wrapped about her, but as she moved to snuggle against him, Glynn evaporated, washed away by sunlight. Katy blinked several times. On the bedside table, the metallic owl's lazy eyelids drooped; weighted by missed sleep as if the owl had watched over her while she slept. Katy sat up, drawing the duvet around her and slipping back to sit in the hollow where Glynn used to sleep. She'd left the owl on the mantelpiece along with her keys.

The owl winked.

Katy threw her pillow at the toy bird, knocking it onto the carpet. Now she couldn't see it and that was somehow worse than having the thing watch her. She rubbed her eyes, feeling irrational and no wonder after the previous day's events. The mattress creaked beneath her. Katy leaned over the side of the bed to find the owl. It sat beside the pillow, blinking at her, perhaps a twitch of a smile to its beak.

Okay, now she was losing her mind. It was just an inanimate object. It didn't have personality or intent. She'd take it back to the tramp and forget about it. Or was that an excuse, a flimsy reason to return to the building? The alarm clock buzzed. Since Glynn's death, she always awoke before the alarm clock sounded. She slammed her hand on it. She couldn't go into work today, too much Glynn swirling about her mind. She had to know that yesterday was an illusion. No, she couldn't go in. She picked up the owl. Its wings vibrated against her palm — just an inanimate object in a world full of fancy.

On her way out the house, Katy tore the doodle from the phone pad and scribbled 'I Love You, Glynn' in red ink beneath the little man with the enormous heart. What harm to carry a piece of Glynn with her? A breadcrumb to lure him back. In her jeans pocket, the owl knocked against her hip. Katy's heart fluttered in time with its wings, sanity drowned in her stomach acid and nerves rose as butterflies in her chest.

Outside The Flats, the shopping trolley continued to roll back and forth. The discarded fruit machine had gained a friend — an old jukebox that vomited broken vinyl. Her world looked the same, if a little dirtier at the edges.

There were no free seats on the bus into town, but although people jostled against her and rucksacks whacked the back of her head and her shoulders, she barely noticed them. She looked through the bus window where she saw shadows of life passing. At the final stop, Katy joined the tide of disembarking passengers. Before turning the corner onto The Strand, Katy drew in a breath. She couldn't decide if she wanted to find Glynn there or not or what she could do about it if she saw Glynn again. The wind encouraged her on, pushing her around the corner, rushing her to the doorway where the tramp sat with his box of things.

When she reached the building, the wind stilled and the traffic faded to a distant roar. The world reduced to what the building may conceal. She pulled the metallic owl from her pocket. It buzzed against her fingertips. Felt now as if it belonged to her and not to the tramp.

"I forgot to ask your name yesterday," Katy said.

He didn't offer it.

"I seem to have this," she said, holding out the owl.

"So you do."

"I don't know how I came to take it. I apologise. Here," Katy said, but he didn't take the owl. "I don't want it."

"It's not about what you want, Katy."

"How do you know my name?"

"You told me. Yesterday. I'm Amos, although that may be a lie. Names are powerful things, Katy, but I am happy to give you something to call me by if it makes things easier for you. Oh, and you might want to stand aside."

"What?"

The wind punched Katy in her lower back, pushing her towards the door. Amos gathered his box of things, unperturbed by the sudden gust. The owl fought against her grip but when she let go, eager to drop it, the owl clung to her palm, its claws caught under her engagement ring. The wind rushed about her, occupied now by a hum of voices offering indistinct words. Somewhere within their chant, she heard her name. Katy spun around. The ghosts headed towards the building, passing around the stilled traffic. Glynn stepped onto the pavement behind a man in a dark grey suit; the man who had watched her from the central reservation the day before. He looked at her now, this man, looked at and pretended to look through. There was no pretence in Glynn's vacant stare.

Amos grabbed her arm, pulling her out of the ghost's path. "Stand aside or be forever buried with them."

"He's here," she said, before the wind stole her voice. Here.

The man in the grey suit nodded to her, "Pleasure to make your acquaintance, I'm Yarker Ryland. Won't you please join us inside for a dusty cup of dried-up tea?"

Despite Amos' grip relaxing about her wrist, Katy didn't step forward. Instead, she shrunk back against the building. Ghosts didn't make conversation with the living. Yarker shrugged and withdrew a key from his pocket and opened the door. The key as ornate as the one Katy had used to open the door the previous day. Then, he stood aside to allow the other ghosts to file into the building. Katy leaned forward, watching as each ghost faded from grey to black within the dark hollow of the doorway. She couldn't allow Glynn to enter and disappear. She reached out. Her fingertips brushed his and didn't pass through; warm fingers, solid, and not at all ghost-like. He drifted away. Amos proved a belt at her waist, pulling her back from the doorway and from Glynn. Glynn disappeared inside the building.

Katy scratched at Amos's fingers until he let go. There was only one ghost left, one ghost and the man named Yarker. She feared that once they entered the door would close and that would be that. What had Amos said yesterday? You have to wait for them to return and open the door for you. Well they'd returned and it was open. The remaining ghost shambled by Katy. He moved discordant with the rest, his ghostly pallor more washed-out than grey. His clothes dishevelled rather than starched. He wore no shoes and only one sock — a yellow and green striped sock to stand out against the grey. More important, he turned and regarded her.

"If you're sure," he said, holding out his hand.

She grabbed his hand. His skin was cold while Glynn's had been warm, his fingers trembled where Glynn's had been steady. She'd never been less sure of anything. He led her into the building and no one objected. She entered the dark and found herself blind; the only light a green exit sign at the far end of the room. The door closed behind her. It took a good few minutes for the dark to settle to gloom and offer indistinct forms and all the time, her breaths grew more panicked. She kept her ground though, aware the door should be within a few steps. As light began to form in the square of window, Katy fumbled for the handle; attempted to turn it.

The door didn't open. Trapped.

Fluorescent lights flickered on, offering a dull grey light. Katy turned to face the ghosts.

SIX

Isobel knew if she was alive and Peter dead she wouldn't play the fool and a) walk into a building full of ghosts and b) bring a boy with her. With her eyes permanently open (never any respite to blink), Isobel noted the way the living woman's shoulder brushed Peter's and how her hand gripped his. Perhaps he thought to make Isobel jealous. If she could work her vocal cords, she'd scream, 'You do know I'm dead.'

Realising his mistake, Peter let go of the girl's hand and drifted to Isobel's desk. She hated how he stared at her, how he reached out and traced her face. She hated the feel of his fingers. She hated how her skin no longer reacted to his touch. Better if he left her to crumble to nothing. Better he allowed her mind to become a jumble of nonsense with no sense of anything for that may be the only death to be found here.

Peter obscured her view of the living woman and Isobel couldn't lean to the side and look around him. After several minutes, she forgot she was Isobel at all. It took Peter's touch to reawaken her. She'd slap him away if she could.

Don't want to remember.... Don't want to remember... Don't want to remember.

There are worse things than being dead. Such as a) remembering you're dead and b) having the living breathing all over you. Peter shifted to the right and now Isobel saw the living woman again. The living woman shuddered. Isobel wished the woman shuddered because of her. If only she could move and give them all a show.

SEVEN

A woman sat behind the reception desk, her hair a bouffant of cobwebs. To Katy, the woman looked like a mannequin. Skin drawn taut over bone, blue veins visible beneath skin, startling against the layer of grey. The bouffant woman didn't look like a ghost; none of them did. The man who'd led Katy into the building stood in front of the reception desk, his hand hovering an inch above the receptionist's hand, as though he thought she would disintegrate at his touch. Before Katy could investigate if the receptionist was real or plastic, the ghost who had opened the door, Yarker Ryland, danced before her. Yarker grabbed Katy's hand and twirled her on the spot. Twirled and twirled and twirled her until she fell, knocking her hip against the side of the reception desk. Then, with a bow, he spun into an open-plan office to her left.

Katy stood and rubbed her hip, wiping dust from her hands onto her jacket.

"I warned you," the boy at the desk said, turning from the mannequin-ghost.

"You didn't." Had he? Katy asked, "What of?"

"I asked if you were sure."

"That's not a warning. Who are you?"

"The same as you more or less with emphasis on the less. My name is Peter. Sorry," he said. "I forget what it's like to be around the living. Niceties and all that"

"Katy. Are you dead?"

"Ha! Not yet. At least, I don't think so. I was alive when I entered and I don't recall dying in between. I get hungry—I steal food. I drink from rain puddles and dripping taps. I suppose I should be dead. Sometimes, I want to be dead. If you're here, I guess you want to be dead too."

Katy shook her head. "No, I..."

"You saw someone."

She nodded.

"Well you'll probably find him in there. That's where all the others are. Good luck Katy, I hope he remembers you."

Katy turned towards the office. I hope he remembers you. Desks were set three columns wide and at least eight rows long. Each desk held a computer. Ghosts sat with their heads bent to the monitors. Smile twitched — seemed there was no escape from the office even in the afterlife. She moved amongst the desks. Glynn sat hunched over a keyboard, his fingers scrolling from screen to screen. He appeared a stranger. Glynn had hated computers and new technology in general. He played vinyl, composed letters on an old Olivetti typewriter, wrote with fountain pens, distrusted microwaves. Although his appearance matched Glynn's, this copy behaved like a stranger. If he was Glynn, why didn't he look at her?

"Glynn?"

Perhaps he thought her an illusion. Having spent so much time with the dead, he may not believe in the living anymore. He was a fever dream to her.

"Is it you, Glynn?"

For a moment, she expected him to look at her and say 'no'. Instead, Glynn continued to stare at the computer screen and its collection of grainy images. It looked as if the ghosts had accessed the city's CCTV system. As she reached to touch Glynn's face, the ghost named Yarker coughed. Katy looked up and away from Glynn. Yarker stood before the windows, the only ghost (apart from the mannequin-receptionist) who didn't work behind a computer. Yarker wagged his finger and shook his head.

"Do not touch your dead," Yarker said.

She leaned forward, her fingers a centimetre away from Glynn's cheek.

"Oh go on then," Yarker said. "If you must."

She drew her hand away. Yarker smiled.

"I am forever grateful for the long hours spent listening to a lecturer lecture about reverse psychology. Now I've confused you. Now you don't know what to do. Should you touch him? Will you explode into dust if you do? Maybe a kiss will waken him from his zombie-like slumber. However, you don't look like the princess sort, more the ugly sister. Apologies, death makes me speak my mind and beauty is in the eye of the beholder etc etc."

"Why are you here?"

"Why are you?" Yarker asked in return. He danced forward. "No... wait, I know the answer to that one. Because of him."

Glynn paused on a CCTV image of a boarded-up launderette. Katy noted that the neighbouring ghosts highlighted the same scene on their monitors. Onscreen, one of the boards covering the launderette doors dropped to the ground revealing a girl trapped within the launderette, a girl in a tattered grey dress. She looked about sixteen. Glynn (and his neighbours) leaned forward, fingers attacking the monitor, sliding across the image until the launderette looked out of proportion. Until it looked as though the building were falling down, the roof too heavy for its crumbling walls. Within the launderette, the girl beat her fists and Lego blocks against the window. Lego blocks.

"What are you doing? What are they doing?"

"So many questions. No wonder Glynn stepped in front of that coach. He wanted a little peace, a little quiet," Yarker said.

"What do you know about Glynn's death?"

Yarker raised an eyebrow, straightened his tie, and looked rather smug.

"Fuck you," she said.

"I admire your bravery. My wife, god rest her soul... please, someone bury her... would have run screaming at the sight of one ghost and yet you stand amongst us and insult the head-honcho, the lead owl. As I like to think of myself. I admire that. No, really I do."

Katy touched Glynn's arm. All the dead turned towards her and, except Glynn, all the dead stood. Chairs scraped back. Scratch. Scratch. Scratch. Katy removed her hand from Glynn's arm. Yarker shook his head.

"Don't touch your dead," Yarker said, wagging his finger.

Don't touch when she wanted to crush Glynn to her, to feel the weight of his arms around her, but this mannequin remained unresponsive. She ached to kiss his cheek.

"Are you him?" Katy asked Glynn.

For thirteen months, she'd wished the world away, had bartered all she owned (including her life) for one more moment with Glynn. This wasn't what she'd asked to exchange her life for. They couldn't stop her touching him. Katy clasped her arms around Glynn's neck and squeezed. She missed the feel of his arms about her. She missed so much about him. This Glynn didn't respond to her touch. He didn't gaze into her eyes or tell her how much he loved her.

"Glynn," she whispered.

The dead encircled them. Their blank expressions turned towards her; empty, grey eyes, betraying neither malevolence nor kindness. Katy's arms remained about Glynn's neck, but her grip loosened. Yarker stood with his back to the window. He controlled these dead. If she could break his hold over them, perhaps Glynn would respond to her touch, perhaps he would remember her. The dead stepped closer leaving no room to escape. Katy pulled away from Glynn. She pressed her hands to her chest as if holding her heart together.

"Why can't I touch him?" she asked Yarker. "What harm can it do? Don't you remember being in love? Did anyone love you? Did anyone love any of you?"

Glynn looked up. Whether he did so because Yarker's invisible strings orchestrated him, she couldn't say. She hoped the word love had resurrected a part of him. It gave her hope. She needed hope. Remember me.

"Love is for the living," Yarker said. "If it bothers you so, die."

The dead relaxed a little. At first, she thought they stepped back to give her more room, but then Glynn's chair pushed back and he stood. The dead had moved so he could join them.

"I'm not an illusion, Glynn. I'm here. I'm real. Remember me."

The dead turned to Yarker awaiting instruction. Katy's fingers hesitated at Glynn's sleeve. Trembled. Yarker shook his head but smiled as he did so. His smile caused her to pull away from Glynn.

"I could order them to tear you apart hair follicle to fingernail to eyeball and limb," Yarker said. "But I'm a gentleman. Or maybe I'm just pulling your leg... off. Ooh, I could order them to do that and then you'd have to crawl out of here. But I don't like blood, which surprises me."

The dead laughed in synch. Shoulders and chests heaving, mouths open, but the laughter didn't reach their eyes. Mid-laugh, Glynn spun on his heels and faced her. No sound escaped his mouth. A dry, cavernous laugh to suck from her what remained of hope.

"No, you don't do this to me. You don't do this to us."

Katy grabbed Glynn's hand. The dead inched closer.

"You're Glynn Cutler and I'm your girlfriend, Katy Seymour. Your fiancée. We should have married last June. It rained that day. Great thunderous clouds."

No response. The dead stare of an emptied man, of a corpse. Maybe he wasn't even here. A fabrication of her grief leaving her as cuckoo as the metallic owl that thought it could fly.

"You're twenty-three, fucking gorgeous and you love drawing, comic books, antiques, and me."

Glynn pulled his hand free from hers. She'd never felt emptier.

"You're not him. You can't be him."

This Glynn was a facsimile. A faded replica. The dead stepped back, gaps opening up between them. She shouldn't have chased after ghosts. Glynn stood amongst the dead, joining their circle.

"He belongs to them, not you," Peter said, standing at the doorway into the office. "They belong to them, not us. You should leave before you find you can't."

"You really should," Yarker said.

The striplights flickered, erasing the dead with each blink. Within the building, they only existed in thin grey light. Katy stepped out of the circle, easing between the dead. Their clothing felt like dust, their skin paper-thin. Glynn didn't follow her escape. The dead reshuffled and began to return to their seats. Phantoms, they passed through desks that were broken one moment and the next held monitors and keyboards. The lights continued to flicker.

"Hurry," Peter said, as if afraid she too would fade.

Glynn had almost vanished. Sunlight poured into the lobby, further stealing the dead, stealing Glynn.

She turned to Glynn. "Come with me." A final, ignored plea.

Risking reanimating the dead, Katy rushed back to Glynn and wrapped her arms around his neck. He didn't smell like her Glynn. He didn't smell of anything. Tears streaming down her cheeks, Katy ran from the room. The receptionist had faded to a sketch, a thin outline of a girl with exaggerated hair. Sunlight erased the receptionist's hands. The front door stood ajar. Katy turned to look into the office a final time. Yarker shivered up to the office doorway. He reached into his pocket and began pulling out a chain that was at first watch-chain thin but the more he pulled, the weightier the chain became. When he had withdrawn it all, he tensed the links between his fists.

"Go," Peter said. "Go and don't look back."

Yarker stepped into the lobby. The ends of the chain scratched worn linoleum, cut into the back of her ankle. Sunlight washed the room behind him, expunging Glynn, expunging everything but Yarker, Peter and herself. The door yawned open, hinges squeaking, then teasing her, it rebounded, closing almost to the frame. Katy ran for the door, shoes skidding through dust. As she slipped between door and frame, the chain bit into her wrist, tethering her to the building. She pulled against its restraint, grimacing against the cut of each link. Her heart pounded. With her free hand, she grabbed the doorframe and managed to pull herself out the building. The door slammed to, cutting through the chain. Its links evaporated.

Amos sat in the doorway, his box of things placed between his knees. Despite the fresh air, the mustiness of the office clung to her skin.

"Are you dead?" she asked.

"Sometimes even the living can be dead. A better question may be, am I alive? And in response to that I'll say, not always."

She pressed her hand to the door. The building gave no hint as to what hid within. So much for offering anything to have Glynn back, she should have dragged him from the building. Even weighted with her grief, a ghost couldn't weigh much.

She took Glynn's doodle from her pocket, where it nestled beside the owl, and slipped the paper halfway beneath the door. Someone pulled the note fully through to the other side. They were still in there.

EIGHT

Nobody escapes death. Yarker wished he'd told Katy that. He stared at her silhouette, her shape, pressed against the door, echoing against its glass. She believed she'd escaped.

"Nobody escapes death," he whispered, lips to the window. Then Yarker spun on his heels and addressed Peter, "You certainly don't escape death. May as well fix a noose to the light fittings and be done. You could be with Isobel then. Twin dolls stuffed to the gut with spiders. Sounds like a plan. I'll wheel another chair into reception for you."

Peter looked at the door, contemplating escape.

"You think it's still possible for you," Yarker said. "Despite your breath, you're one of us now. The world would rip you apart. Ooh, on second thoughts, do try to escape. A dismembering would brighten this grey day."

"She's gone," Peter said, his inadequate chin poking at Yarker.

"Isobel or the living girl? No matter, you're wrong on both counts. I do like that you're always wrong it makes me feel so right."

Yarker leaned across the reception desk and stared into Isobel's eyes. He rapped his knuckles against her forehead and relished her scream. A scream audible only to him for Isobel remained trapped within her corpse.

"Wake up, sleepyhead," Yarker said. "Or, I'll huff and I'll puff and I'll crack your skull open."

"Leave her alone," Peter said, attempting to grab Yarker's arm. Peter's hand passed through supposed sleeve and skin.

To the living, the dead could be corporeal or mist. To the dead, those living were a common enemy. Tugging on Isobel's cobweb bouffant, Yarker drew the girl up until she balanced on unsteady legs, her puppet arms dripping by her sides. Yarker spun her around, then let go. Peter rushed around the desk to catch her and her dust. Her bones landed on him, knocking Peter to the floor, pinning him.

"Get a room," Yarker said, and danced back into the office.

Behind Yarker, Peter began to cry.

*

Her Peter lay beneath her, his body shaking from the weight of tears, from grief. If she could move her limbs without Yarker's help, she'd wrap her hands around his neck and throttle the life from him. The final crumbs of her love for him disintegrated. How dare he feel sorry for himself when she was the one trapped in a broken body waiting for Yarker to bury her soul along with her corpse? He had breath, he had hope, he had the ability to love, to grieve. Although... Isobel assumed she grieved too. For herself. She missed laughing. She missed loving this man.

If she'd loved him.

An image flashed of her arms wrapped around Peter's neck, her lips pressed to his, the spread of warmth, of tingling flesh. Beneath her, Peter squirmed. He pushed against her shoulders and rolled her off him. Now, Isobel lay on her back staring glass-eyed at the ceiling.

Forget... Forget... Forget.

Isobel's left hand twitched. Perhaps a mouse burrowed beneath it. Perhaps Yarker worked an animation spell. Perhaps she was coming back. As Peter struggled to lift her into the chair, Isobel tested her fingers and wondered when they would be strong enough to strangle.

*

Yarker gathered almost all his dead to him. They swarmed and clustered, pressing their corporeal forms together allowing their ghost edges to blend until they were almost indistinguishable from each other. Yarker gathered almost all his dead with the exception of Isobel. With great effort, Peter had positioned Isobel in her chair and rolled said chair to the desk to keep her upright.

Now, Peter slumped against the wall, back pressed to the lifts. Yarker knew Peter wanted to force open the doors, to fall into the empty shaft and break. They'd worn him to almost nothing. Yarker danced free of his entourage and led them towards Peter and the lift. Peter's back straightened, aware of the vulnerability of his situation. The dead wanted to push Peter down the lift shaft. They whispered of their intent to Yarker, Isobel's cry loudest of all. Oh, the living did not understand their dead at all. Concentrating on the lift doors, Yarker forced them open. Peter teetered at the edge, attempting to keep his balance by means of flapping his arms and squeaking. Well it sounded like a squeak to Yarker.

As Peter began to topple backwards, Yarker wrapped his arm around Peter's waist and saved him from falling into the shaft. The dead cried as one. The dead continued to press. They wanted Peter dead. They wanted Katy dead. They wanted to strip the world bare until only skeletons of buildings and of men remained.

NINE

In her thirteen months of grieving, Katy believed if she saw Glynn again she would never let him go. Then, she'd done just that. Sitting in their bedroom, she tried not to think of them together, of when Glynn was alive. Memory hurt too much. A hatbox containing a pink veil lay open on the bed. It smelled of roses, of must, and of things supposed lost. Some days, Katy thought she would crumble to dead dreams in this terraced house, would become a ghost while others moved in around her, filling its walls with life again. Now there was the smallest possibility she could have that life again or as near to it as she dared to hope.

The telephone rang downstairs. Katy pulled the veil with her, hugging it to her chest as she ran down the stairs. The telephone's LCD offered Steph's number.

"Hey, Steph."

"You okay? We've been worried about you?"

Katy's pitch upped. "Of course."

"You haven't seen him again? I mean, thought you've seen him again. Glynn," Steph asked, tagging Glynn's name to the end of the sentence as if they could have been talking about anyone else.

"I'm sorry I worried you."

"It's been over a year, Kate."

Thirteen months, thirteen days.

"I don't believe there's a time limit on such things. Except those which other people impose."

"We care about you. You're not alone in this."

Lie. No matter how often people sympathised or offered an interested ear they couldn't hold her in bed or whisper they loved her, at least not in the way Glynn had. Katy draped the veil across her face and stared at her ghost reflection in the vestibule door.

"I'll meet you in the pub on Friday. You'll see I'm fine. I just had a blip and blips are allowed. It's in the manual."

"There's a manual."

Katy laughed.

Steph said, "I did not just ask that. Please erase all mention of manuals."

After their call ended, with further promises from Katy that she knew she hadn't seen Glynn, Katy stood by the vestibule door staring at the image of a bride caught within it. Could she marry a dead man? She'd marry Glynn whether he was dead or not. A deceased vicar could preside. One more kiss. Behind her, something thudded against the kitchen window. She spun around. Another thud, and this time, having moved into the living room, she saw something hit the yard wall. She lifted the veil.

The yard door swung open into the back street. Katy stepped into the yard closing the kitchen door behind her. A shadow stretched across the back street, as though someone hid just out of view. Katy's heart thudded. In her yard, Lego pieces lay scattered across pitted concrete — yellow and white blocks on a green board, the remains of a house still attached with hollow spaces for windows and its door hanging from a single hinge. She recalled the ghost in the launderette and the blocks it had bashed against the window. What connection could that have to this? Clouds shivered across the sun, obliterating the lurking shadow.

She should bolt the door, instead she asked, "Glynn?" Why would Glynn throw a Lego house into their yard?

Why would anyone?

The back street proved to be empty. Of course, someone could crouch behind a bin or maybe they'd scaled the railings and were hiding in the remnants of the old, abandoned school at the rear of her house. There was also the possibility they hid in a neighbour's yard. Yes, she should bolt the door and scurry back to their bedroom and to memory. The breeze tugged at her veil causing pink netting to drape over her face. Along the back street, an old metal bin fell and clattered into the gutter. Rotten vegetables spilled and rolled into the road. As Katy lifted her veil, someone or something threw a mouldy carrot. Someone or something she couldn't see. The carrot splattered against the school wall. Katy hesitated. She stared at the air between the carrot and the bin and tried to make out grey shadows.

A potato cut across the air and slammed into her shoulder, its rotten juices dripping from the veil.

"Glynn," she whispered.

The air shimmered, offered indistinct outlines of things. She couldn't determine if Glynn stood amongst them. If he did, surely the potato was a warning and if he warned her to run, then he still cared. Another potato flew, spattered against her breast. Heart fluttered. Katy ran back to the house and slammed the backyard door and the kitchen door. It would be a warning, not hate. Glynn could never hate her. She could never hate him. Tearing off the ruined veil, Katy sat on the bed and drew her knees to her chest. Sobs shuddered through her body; tears soaked her face and hands. She'd thought nothing could be worse than losing Glynn, but then she'd never entertained the possibility he wouldn't want her anymore. It couldn't be true. Yet, the evidence proved otherwise. Outside her room, a stair creaked.

"Just the house settling," she said.

Perched on the edge of their bed, Katy waited for another stair to creak, for shadow to curve and slide into her room. The silence hurt. After a moment or two, she climbed from the bed, wincing as springs twanged and floorboards creaked. In three steps, she stood at the top of the landing and peered not at ghost or man but at the remains of the Lego house, which now balanced on the bottom stair. Paper poked from its doorway. She hesitated on the top step. The Lego house could be a mousetrap to lure her downstairs. Common sense insisted if they wanted to hurt her they could do so as easily if she was upstairs, they did not need to lure.

Crouched on the second stair, she placed the Lego house

on her knee and removed the note. Unravelling it, she noted Glynn's doodle of the little man, heart erupting from his chest, and underneath the sketch her declaration of love, but there was something else now, an extra written in pencil — sometimes they shouldn't come back.

TEN

Peter pitied Katy. With a scrap of paper clutched to her chest, she peered from her bedroom window and looked across an empty street, trying to see that which hid from her. Peter understood the torment of wanting to see and not see your dead. He decided — too late now — the note had been a mistake. That the Lego house with its symbolic 'your world comes tumbling down' could strike hope rather than fear.

There was no hope amongst the dead. There was only the want to die, the want to forget who you were and whom you once loved. There was no space for love in death.

The dead tugged at him, pulling him towards the abandoned cinema. Abandoned by the living not the dead. He understood a little of their hate now. Correction, he understood a lot of it. He had lost. Worse, he had lost and regained. Katy faded from his view, as if she were the ghost. There may still be a chance for her. Then again, there probably wasn't.

Within the cinema, Peter clambered over broken seats and dislodged bricks; the soles of his feet ravaged by weeks of wearing no shoes and spending time in disused places. His ankles ached from holding up a body that would rather curl in a corner until breath expunged. He should have remained lying beneath Isobel.

He shouldn't have pushed her immobile body off him. He did not say corpse. He did not think corpse. They were not corpses. He didn't know what they were, although sometimes he hoped they were not the dead, that they were illusions gathered together by grief.

ELEVEN

With the metallic owl in her pocket and the veil, now washed and dried, trailing from the waistband of her jeans, Katy left the house and set out to kidnap Glynn. She would use the veil to tie him to her so either she remained with the dead or he came back to the living. Either way, she would not lose him again; even if he didn't remember her.

The metal shutters, which had covered the cinema door, lay scattered across the pavement. A broken cinema seat, its yellowed stuffing drifting along concrete, wobbled beside it. Sounds echoed from within the cinema — tinny laughter and things breaking, the inhuman cry of a building screaming against the dismantling of its insides. More unnerving, her name echoed within the cries. The dead were in the cinema. The dead waited for her.

Katy climbed over debris. The dark inside the cinema was complete, offering no hint of shadow or outline of her hand. In the distance, the tobacco factory whistle blew. She hadn't heard its siren in years, not since the factory had closed. Laughter slid from the darkness. Katy turned to look out at the day and wondered why the sunlight didn't cross the threshold. The sharp light stung her eyes. The laughter fell back, replaced by her name whispered through familiar lips. Glynn.

On turning, she found the darkness lessened, reduced to a washed-out image. Someone stood ahead. She could make out their outline but not their features. They faded in and out like a static picture struggling to tune in.

"Hello," she said.

Her fingers curled around the owl in her pocket. Its wings vibrated. Behind her, metal screeched. She spun on her heels. Pinpricks of light pushed through tin. Someone had replaced the shutter over the doorway, locking her in the cinema. Despite the reduced daylight, the inside of the cinema lightened albeit with a grey cast. Double doors, which hung off their hinges, led into the auditorium where the dead tore at rotten curtains, hurled broken cinema seats at the screen and hung from the crumbling balcony pulling at the frescos. None of these dead mattered for the figure standing against the wall, black stains fanning either side of him to form wings, was Glynn. He looked at her. She couldn't look away from him. The building could crumble about her and she wouldn't willingly move.

Glynn stepped away from the wall and from the angel wing graffiti, which she'd mistaken for stains. The graffiti artist's tag cut down the spine — Glynn Cutler. As he moved away from the wall, she moved towards it. Instead of chasing him, she chased his art, tracing her fingers along each feather, along his name, along its/his spine. Had he drawn the wings before or after death? She hoped after. That way it confirmed something of her Glynn remained.

The Overseer appeared on stage gathering the dead to him. He appeared a dark blot against the torn screen. His arm stretched out, fingers pointing towards Katy. The dead turned to her, Glynn amongst them. Their features erased. Grey canvases waiting for an artist to determine their degree of beauty. If they shuffled, she'd lose Glynn amongst the faceless dead. She shouldn't have followed them in.

"No you shouldn't," Yarker said.

Katy startled. She tried to empty her mind but the more she tried the more thought turned over. He couldn't have read her mind. Of course, none of this should be possible. Only rational explanation — she'd lost her mind. If so, let her mind weave this into a pleasanter tale.

Yarker grinned and said, "Now I may not let you leave."

Peter, the boy who walked with the dead, stepped from the crowd. He still wore his face unlike the featureless dead. Peter looked almost as grey as them but in a sick rather than a ghostly fashion. The only colour to his pallor was a scratch running down his cheek, burning red against dirt.

"Peter, would you do anything to get your Isobel back?" Yarker asked.

Peter began to nod and then hesitated. "That would depend."

"Oh, don't worry. I'm not threatening your life, I am threatening dear Katy's."

Katy stepped back. The uneven floor caused her to lose her balance and she turned her ankle. She bit against the pain. She wouldn't run. Heck, she probably couldn't run now. Katy steadied herself against a pillar, paint peeling beneath the sweat of her palm. She'd never been good at running.

"I'm not afraid of you. You're ghosts. You're forgotten things and far easier to bury than... me." This was probably not true.

"That would be your cue to run," Yarker said.

"I won't hurt you," Peter said. "At least, I'll try not to."

Yarker clapped and jumped from the stage. "He'll try. Such a trooper. He'll try not to snap your neck or smash your skull against the wall. He'll probably fail but at least you'll know he tried not to murder you. Or... I could have Glynn do it instead. Sometimes it's harder to see the face you love just before you die, especially when it's snarling and rabid. How awful to be murdered by the man you trusted most of all."

"Glynn would never hurt me."

"You should never have faith in anyone but yourself. It's a lesson I learned while dangling from an open window."

For all his monstrous words, this man once feared death. These were all people who had lived and loved and if she could find their living perhaps they would find peace. The blank visages of the dead shivered until their features returned. Glynn smirked.

She stepped back, watching her footing. Falling over could murder her. She backed towards the tin door, hoped someone hadn't nailed it down or other ghosts didn't press against it. The dead clustered and moved into the foyer with Yarker at the head.

"I won't hurt you," Peter repeated, but he didn't seem so sure.

She would do dreadful things to win Glynn back. She must not contemplate the rewards either.

"My, my, my," Yarker said, again as if he'd read her thoughts. "Perhaps we could reverse things and you could strangle Peter. I've been waiting weeks for him to lie in front of a car or jump from somewhere high and go splat. People so very rarely go splat these days."

The gap between Katy and the dead lengthened. The door had to be close. She kept on retreating until her back hit the wall and light pushed through tin to her left.

"No, don't escape," Yarker said, standing on tiptoes and leaning forward as though stretching to grab her wrist, but in reality making no effort at all. "We want you to stay. Glynn wants you to stay."

Katy turned and pushed at tin. The sound of the factory clock's whistle blew through the door and echoed around the ruined cinema. With a thump, she pushed the tin shutter forward and fell with it into the street. Metal cut into her knee. The world blurred behind tears, breath hitched in her throat. She couldn't stay here, nor could she go home. Knowing Glynn existed in the world, she'd not settle to grieving, to moving on with her life. Whatever the consequences, she wouldn't let him go. If she could hold onto him in daylight, perhaps she could steal him home, perhaps the dead only held sway over him in the dark, in this grey light. Behind her, the dead began to file from the cinema.

TWELVE

"Grief tastes like salty butter," Yarker said. "Go bite the girl and let me know if that's true. The dead have no taste buds. "

When Peter didn't answer, Yarker added, "Do I have to put on every goddamn show?"

THIRTEEN

Katy sat between worlds. Perched on a cinema chair on Boaler Street, Katy watched the dead file from the cinema while the living drove by — all spectres. If she moved, she would fall into one world or the other. She wasn't certain which she wanted more. Yellow foam (seat stuffing) drifted about her ankles, the only real thing in this insubstantial world. Yarker, Peter and Glynn were last to exit the cinema.

If she had a smart phone she'd Google 'Yarker Ryland' to see if there were any articles about his death. Perhaps he would prove as mad in life as in death. Of course, if he turned out to be real that meant Glynn wasn't a figment of her imagination. She would need someone else to verify the Google hits. Imagination was tricky like that.

Peter approached with his hand outstretched. If she took it, would she fade against the backdrop of the cinema? Would she become a ghost? She looked over Peter's shoulder at Glynn. Glynn stared at her. She couldn't read the intent in his smile. He appeared a stranger. She stood and took Peter's hand.

He felt warm.

He felt alive.

They joined the rank and file of the dead. So she'd made a choice. Glynn moved ahead of them, leading the pack along with Yarker. Her knee smarted where she'd scraped it against tin. As they passed The Flats, the shopping trolley continued its roll back and forth, but now Katy saw that a girl balancing a toddler on her hip pushed said trolley. Ghosts.

"You're not dead either," Katy said to Peter, both of them watching the ghost girl and her child.

Amongst the dead, Katy and Peter shivered by The Flats and the children's playground, reaching West Derby Road in what seemed only a couple of steps. Walking amongst the dead gave her giant steps, an ease to her stride, each footstep also left her feeling further from home. The usual busy intersection at West Derby Road was deserted. Yarker stood on the grass verge between lanes. He held out his arms, turned to the group and gave a sweeping bow. Colours warped — greens, blues and browns streaking as though the world was a watercolour painting and it had just begun to rain. The ground shifted. Katy's grip tightened within Peter's.

When the world had ceased its blur, Katy found they'd transferred to some place other. They queued outside the office building on The Strand. Her limbs shook, wasted, as though she'd raced the distance between home and town.

"How did we get here?" Katy asked.

"They brought us with them."

Of course they had. Amos sat to the right of the doorway. He didn't look at her and perhaps he couldn't see her amongst the dead. She examined her hand, relieved to find it wasn't grey. He pecked through the contents of the box — a pink cocktail umbrella, blocks and a cigarette case. The owl flapped in Katy's pocket, its metallic wings buzzing. Katy wanted to fly too; instead, she shuffled by Amos and his box of things and entered the building along with the dead. She didn't even have time to ask Amos his purpose in this. It took a moment for the dark to fade to grey; she found she saw well enough in it now.

Peter stood before the reception desk. "We were to be married."

He scratched at a tattoo inked on the inside of his wrist. Within the office, the dead wore grins the copy of Yarker's tight-lipped smile. They leaned forward in synch, losing themselves in the grainy city images that darted across their screens.

"You shouldn't have followed us," Peter said, perhaps forgetting he had taken her hand and led her with them. "Although your return was inevitable. No one escapes them."

"What are they?"

Peter frowned.

"I mean, are they our dead or some malevolent facsimile?"

Mostly, Katy wanted to know why Glynn didn't recognise her. Perhaps he thought to drive her away, to save her. Peter shrugged.

"Does it matter?" he asked.

"Of course it matters. I have Glynn back or am this" — she pinched her fingers together — "close to having him back. How can you be so passive?"

Peter snorted. "Give it time."

He held out his arm to show the inside of his wrist. The skin was puckered, looking sore, around a rectangular tattoo that read 'Property of the Bureau of Them, Us and You.'

"I don't get to escape them now. Why fight when there's no battle you can win?

"They gave you that tattoo?"

He nodded.

"It doesn't look permanent. More something you could wash off. That doesn't tie you to them."

Ridiculous idea.

"Doesn't it? They're desperate to destroy the world brick by brick. When we're out, when I'm with them, their rage fills me. I'd pull the world apart if I could. Isobel is my anchor; the only thing keeping me alive."

"How did you find her?"

"How you found him."

Isobel watched them from behind the reception desk. Plastic limbs forced into a sitting position, head and back bowed beneath the weight of her bouffant. In recreating Peter's dead, they'd done a poor job. In the office, Yarker slid between aisles.

"You say I'm passive, but at least I ran. Yarker dragged me from the train station, pulled me through abandoned tunnels and this" — Peter again showed his tattoo — "ensures I never escape. They find ways to bind us to them. Beyond those we love that is." He looked at Isobel. "Loved."

Katy shuddered.

Peter slammed his fist against the reception desk. Leaning across the desk, he grabbed Isobel's face. "Why don't you see me, Izzy? I saw you even when you weren't there."

Katy could echo that sentiment. Yarker stood in the doorway, drawn by Peter's outburst.

"They found her in the hotel bathtub," Peter said, wiping snot from beneath his nose. "She slipped; hit her head on the rim. She drowned the morning of our wedding in a hotel just up the road. Sometimes I think this can't be Isobel because when I found her in that tub, the back of her head had caved in. This girl... this girl is almost perfect."

Peter tore the veil from Katy's pocket. Before she could steal it back, he placed it over Isobel's face.

"I never got to see her in her wedding dress."

"I did," Yarker said, winking. "I'd have topped myself too if I looked like she did."

"She didn't kill herself."

Katy looked into the office. All the dead, with the exception of Glynn, concentrated on their screens. Glynn looked across at Katy. Did he recognise her? Yarker shivered up to her, pushing between Katy and Peter.

"Do you mind?" she said.

"Not at all." Yarker bowed and stepped aside. "Apologies for your friend, but he does bore me at times. Make sure you never bore me." Peter had frozen, wound down like a clockwork toy; eyes vacant and chin drooped and resting on his chest. Yarker clicked his fingers. Peter didn't respond.

"Oops," Yarker said. "No, wait. I meant to do that. Delete the oops."

"What have you done?"

Yarker pressed himself against Katy, forcing her to back up until she was jammed against the lift door and him. His breath tasted of week-old chicken left to rot in the sun. She figured he shouldn't have breath at all.

"Were you slaughtered in a meat factory?" she asked.

His cheek muscles tightened; lips and eyes offered a scowl. "I believe I told you how I died. Or maybe I didn't. Window, dangling... ringing any bells? Pay attention. Someone wants to kill you here and I may not be talking about me."

"Did you slaughter yourself in a meat factory?"

Glynn had not committed suicide. Whatever witnesses said about how he walked into the traffic, she knew Glynn and he wasn't capable of taking his own life. Besides, why would he want to? He had her.

Yarker grinned. Again, as if he'd read her mind. Or saw the pain in her eyes. Katy lifted her chin and met him attitude to attitude. She would not cower before this monster; he could do no worse to her than the world already had.

"You're one of us now," Yarker said. "You follow. You think of me as the Pied Piper, dragging your feet to my tune."

"Never."

In the office, the dead stood. They filed into the lobby and gathered at the door. Yarker turned on his heels and skipped to the head of the group. She'd not become his puppet. Partially reanimated, Peter pushed by her to join the dead. He walked stiff, his gait unnatural. The doors onto The Strand opened. Once they'd left she'd search the building, log onto their computers and try

THE BUREAU OF THEM

to figure out the truth of the place and of them. Isobel wouldn't disturb her. Hopefully, she wouldn't disturb Isobel. Glynn hesitated in the doorway. He turned. He waited. She wouldn't go to him.

His hand remained outstretched. "Katy," he said. "You came back to me, Katy."

She'd misheard. He hadn't spoken to her. He didn't recognise her. A trick. Glynn blocked the doorway, making it impossible for the remaining dead to leave. They turned to her, Peter amongst them.

"Katy," Peter said.

"Katy, please," Glynn said.

Behind the desk, Isobel whispered, "Katy, don't."

FOURTEEN

The factory whistle blew.

Through a veil of pink netting, Isobel watched her world empty. The pink cast added no warmth to dead skin. Her neck creaked, a smidgen of movement. If she concentrated on each joint perhaps she could rise from the chair and stumble after the dead. She owned rage too. So much that it threatened to crack skin and sanity. If she wore skin? If this was sanity? It may all be the dream of a decomposing brain trapped in a worm-riddled coffin. Peter may be living his life away from here. She should want that.

She'd rather Peter were dead than his arms were wrapped round someone else.

Fist punched out. A sudden movement not previously experienced in this dead form. Isobel tried to pull her arm back but it remained outstretched, fist clenched so tight her fingers would snap. She would break free of whatever spell Yarker had cobwebbed about her. She stared at her outstretched arm. It took a moment to recognise the delicious movement of the twitch of her left eyelid, a pulse of life where death should be.

The last of the dead (accompanied by a heart that beat) stepped through the doorway and back into the world. Isobel wanted to escape to the places she'd haunted in life, return so she could destroy those who had buried her.

How dare they decide she was done?

They should have laid her to rest in a glass coffin. They should have waited for her breath to mist the glass or for her eyelids to flutter open.

Before leaving, the living woman turned and looked at Isobel. Katy. The girl's name was Katy but Isobel didn't know how she knew that.

"Katy, don't," Isobel said, the words scratching against her throat.

Katy, don't what?

FIFTEEN

The moment Katy joined the swell of the dead Glynn let go of her hand; turned away from her; treated her as a stranger. She wanted to hope it was a survival mechanism — although survival was an oxymoron in his situation. The world faded to a stream of colours, the dizzying sweep of the dead carrying her away. Then the world righted itself (or as near to as it could). They'd arrived at their destination.

They always had a destination.

Katy stood in a perfect bubble of stillness while around her chaos unfolded. The dead crashed into a dilapidated three-storey house. The door swung from its hinges, creaking against the invasion. Windows smashed on the second floor. None of it touched her. She stood as if caught between two worlds. She could feel the warmth of the streetlight above her although its light had extinguished along with the lights in all the houses along the road, occupied and unoccupied. She stood on the edge of the world, boxed in, unable to step back into her world where the living continued unaware of their dead.

Peter hadn't followed the dead into the house. He stood on a patio of sorts with cracked paving slabs and hip-height weeds and kicked at a wheelie bin until it tipped and spilled its contents. He dropped to his knees. She wanted to go to him, to pull him away and bring him back to himself. To do that, she'd have to enter their world and she wouldn't lose herself to their anger as Peter had done. She wouldn't stay among the dead. Glynn didn't want her. Glynn didn't need her. Heck, he probably wasn't even her Glynn — just some copy, some fake boy, some illusion. Katy stepped off the pavement and into the road. The wind slapped against her calves and thighs as a car swerved — a car that hadn't been there a moment before.

"You don't get to leave," Peter said, standing. "We're in their world now."

No. She was in the same world she'd always inhabited and there would be a way home. Peter ran up the steps and disappeared inside the house. He may have allowed the dead to infect him, but she wouldn't stay amongst the dead, she couldn't. She looked along the road. There was no sign of the car now, no traffic at all. Stillness.

"I'm leaving," she said.

Peter shrugged. "If you say so." A window shattered, raining glass on the street, on Katy and Peter.

"If you say so," Peter repeated, and then ran up the stairs and punched into the house.

Legs shaking, Katy ran too, fled up the street determined to put as much space between her and the dead. A stitch nagged at her side. She stopped, rested her hand against a lamp-post, its rough gravelled surface sharp against her palm. Caught her breath. To her left a door opened and a man stepped out of a three-storey house that had been converted to flats. Paint peeled from the doorway. The man looked along the street, his gaze resting on the house the dead destroyed. He jogged down the front steps.

"What's going on there?" the man shouted.

The light emitting from his house drew Katy in, its brightness a sharp contrast to the other houses, all of which remained in darkness and appeared uninhabited. Here was a corner of her world, its glow a possible passage back to streets where the dead did not play. The man stood to the left of the steps and didn't complain when she climbed them. Along the street, a wooden chair tumbled from an upstairs window, shattering on the pavement below. Warmth enveloped her arms. She hadn't even realised she was cold. She'd stand in his hallway and if he complained and threatened to call the police then that would mean she still lived, that the dead did not have her.

The dead roared from the house they'd destroyed and offered the night whoops and hollers. The man fell back, hand clutching his chest. He stumbled up the steps.

"Shoo," he said to Katy. "I want no part of this."

As he stepped into the house, the warm glow faded to a grey

dead-light. The man fell against the newel post, back sliding down it until he sat alongside his corpse.

"No," Katy said.

This man was to be her salvation, her way home. He couldn't be dead. Her heart thudded, drowning out the victorious cries of the dead. Katy raced down the steps and up the road, searching for traffic, for any signs of life. A car engine snarled. Katy stopped, tried to determine from which direction the noise was coming. It had come from her left and from an old car parked on bricks, its rusting engine exposed to the air. The car's engine revved and its body nudged forward, front chassis dropping off bricks. No ghost sat in the driver's seat. No corpse intent on running her over.

The car jolted again, aiming its bumper at Katy's shins. She stepped back. Metal screeched. Flames sparked. The car dropped fully onto the pavement and began to crawl. For a moment, Katy froze. It couldn't hurt her, she thought. It was going too slow for that, she hoped. All it could offer was a need for a tetanus injection. She was safe. The hood popped open, gnashing its metal to gobble her up. She backed up and turned the corner. A metallic chorus joined the scrape and screech of the car.

She stood outside a car scrapyard. With a piercing shriek, the gates creaked open. The tower of cars began to dismantle.

Yarker materialised beside Katy and pushed her into the scrapyard. The gates clanged shut. Behind her, cars began to fall, their metal smashing onto concrete and ricocheting about the yard. A rusting bumper flew towards her face. Katy ducked but it grazed her arm leaving an orange welt in her skin.

"I don't like to hurt folk," Yarker said, from the other side of the gates. "Oh wait, I guess I do."

Katy rattled the gates, trying to unlock that which had no

padlock. The gates fastened together by magnets or fixed with superglue. A wing mirror slammed into her lower back. The dead gathered outside the gates, surrounding Yarker. Peter stepped from their group. Glynn pulled him back, hand fastened around Peter's wrist. Katy turned. A broken collection of cars began to scrape their way across tarmac. They'd crush her to the gates.

No, they wouldn't, Katy decided. She'd clamber over them. Tear them apart.

"All you have to do is agree to come with them," Peter said.

All she had to do. Katy shook her head. Peter smiled at that.

"Think of the little children who will skip by this yard on their way to school. Do you want them to see your innards hanging from open bonnets or oozing through grilles? Do you really intend to allow your severed head to grin at them from a passenger seat?" Yarker said. "Ooh, I'll stay and watch. I'll enjoy their reactions. Maybe prod a few of the blighters into the middle of the road."

The cars creaked closer, forming a half-moon, blocking her in. If they rammed as one she'd be skewered, flattened, one of the gang. Her heart pounded, blood rushed, sounds thudding through her ears to drown out the rev of dead engines. There was no way through the dismantled weave of cars. Katy turned, hooked her fingers into the chainlink gates and began to climb.

"Oh that's not very sporting of you," Yarker said.

A rusting white van slammed into the gates. Despite vibrations from the collision trembling through her fingers and arms, Katy clung onto the gates and continued to climb. At the top, she hesitated. The drop would land her amongst the dead. There was no other choice. Hooking her leg over the top of the gate, regaining her balance as the white van recommenced its attack, she began to clamber down the gate, dropping to the pavement and avoiding the slam of metal on metal. The gates crashed open. The dead did not run. Yarker pressed his hands to the car bonnet, stilling its engine.

"Do you still want him?" Yarker asked.

Katy assumed he meant Glynn. She didn't answer.

"Although, the question should be does he still want you?"

Moving away from the gates but not leaving the vicinity of the dead, Katy turned her back to Yarker. Her stomach churned. Glynn no longer wanted her. Glynn no longer remembered her or cared who she was. No one should know this about their dead.

SIXTEEN

They returned to The Strand. Glynn stood before her, Peter to her left. She wanted to trace Glynn's neckline. She'd lie awake in bed and trace his stubble, giggle as he scratched where she'd touched. Now she was a different sort of irritant. Inside the building, Peter resumed his position by Isobel's desk and the dead settled to work at their computers. Yarker walked amongst the dead.

"Do you still want her?" Katy asked Peter.

Isobel looked to have shifted in her seat. The dust about her disturbed, cobwebs disarranged, veil shifted. Goosebumps peppered Katy's arms. They peppered Isobel's too.

"She doesn't know me." Peter paused. "Yes."

Katy looked at Isobel but detected no movement. Glassy eyes stared through pink netting.

"I'm sorry I found Glynn again." There she'd said it.

In the office, Yarker stopped and turned. Although he should be too far away to hear her, Katy knew he had. He grinned. Did he think he'd won something? Stupid dead zombie-ghost.

Peter scratched at the tattoo on his wrist — Property of the Bureau of Them, Us, and You. He said, "I feel the same."

At Peter's words, there was definite disturbance to the cobwebs dangling from Isobel's fringe.

"I think she's a habit. Something I expect to want. Someone."

Katy stole back her veil, brushing off cobweb silk. She stared at Isobel, daring her corpse-eyes to blink. Isobel played rigor-mortis well. Katy clicked her fingers in front of Isobel's face.

"Leave her be," Peter said.

Someone tapped Katy on the shoulder. Sharp fingernails. She turned. Yarker grinned, black lips painted onto flaking white skin. She wanted to swat him. A good kick and maybe he'd crumble to the dust he should have long ago become. Yarker dug into his pocket and withdrew a self-inking stamp. He placed the stamp on the reception desk, winking at Isobel as he did. He rolled up his jacket sleeves and flexed his fingers.

"No," Peter said. "No, I won't allow it to happen."

"Who were you?" Katy asked Yarker. "I bet you were a coward. I bet your blood ran yellow when you died."

Yarker picked up the stamp and slammed it against the desk. The Property of Them, Us, and You inked onto pale wood. Outside the building, echoing in the frosted glass door, people passed by. A car horn beeped. A lorry hissed as it stopped at the lights, the container it carried reflected in the window. The world waited for her, a step or five away from this monstrous man. She could leave. Of course, she could leave. The Glynn she'd known would expect her to and this new Glynn didn't matter at all. Yarker grabbed her wrist.

"Hey."

The chatter outside the building increased in number and volume. Exhaust fumes travelling on cold air slipped under the door. Yarker pressed the stamp onto her wrist.

"Ow."

The Property of Them, Us, and You. Katy pulled her arm away from him. She spat on the ink and rubbed the edge of her jacket across it until her skin burned. The stamp remained. The echoes of her living world faded.

"This doesn't mean I belong here."

She shook her arm. The tattoo did not slide off. Yarker placed the stamp into his pocket, turned on his heels and crept back to his dead. Katy rubbed her wrist. She marched after Yarker, pushing by him to get to Glynn. He would react to what was happening to her. He would care. She shoved her wrist and its tattoo into Glynn's face. He looked through her hand as if she were the ghost.

"You'll remember who I am. You'll remember who you were," her voice cracked.

She grabbed his arm. A lead weight determined to drop back to the table.

"You have no idea who I am. I bet you're not even him."

Glynn looked up. "I'm him."

A perfect bullet to kill her. I'm him. Yet, she kept breathing.

"I don't need you to want me, Glynn. I want you to remember yourself. This isn't you. Don't play his puppet. You were never anyone's puppet."

Katy wiped snot from beneath her nose. Her wrist itched. Glynn returned to silence as if he'd never spoken. Maybe she'd imagined it. Sure sounded like him. Colder though.

She turned to Yarker. Said, "I'm leaving."

He raised an eyebrow, tapped his feet not in impatience, more in dance.

Katy kissed Glynn's forehead. "I'll never forget you."

This was it then. Without further words, she turned and marched towards reception. Did Yarker or Glynn realise she was leaving? Would either attempt to stop her? Tears ran down her cheeks. She kept her head high, her chin tense, with no wobble to her steps. In the foyer, she pulled at the door. It would open. It had to open.

It didn't open.

She'd smash the glass. In a dark corner, to the right of the lifts, Katy found a plant pot containing a decaying yucca tree. She tipped out the plant and its dry soil, hurled the pot at the door. It rebounded. She picked it up and threw it again, and again, and again, until the pot cracked and shattered into several pieces. A shadow stood on the street side of the door, hands cupped to the glass.

Katy banged her fists against the door. "I'm trapped."

"It's just him," Peter said. "It's just the tramp."

The shadow spread, pressed against glass until it was a dark blot and nothing human at all. She'd find a back exit. A green exit sign blinked above a door to the left of the dead lifts. The bulb sparked offering intermittent light. Behind the door were a stairwell and a fire escape door. Katy's breath hitched. Her fingers curled around the bar that locked the door, metal cold and rusting. She pressed on the bar. Cold air drifted around her ankles. A hand gripped her shoulder, fingers squeezing.

"Katy-Kate."

Glynn. No, he didn't get to do this to her now. At his words, her fingers slipped away from the door. The trick would be to trap her—you don't get to leave. She'd double bluff. Pull Glynn out into the world with her.

"Glynn."

"Katy-Kate."

The fire exit door slammed. Already faint light died, plunging them into darkness. Glynn pulled away. She reached out but couldn't find him. Another door clicked shut but she hadn't seen it open into the foyer. He'd gone. That much she knew. Katy turned and fumbled until her fingers found cold, rusting metal. She pushed down the bar and stepped into the street. I loved you.

Although the door should empty onto the back alley or at least a side street, Katy found herself on The Strand and just outside the building's main doors. The usually busy thoroughfare, a main arterial road into and out of the city, stood silent, empty. She hadn't escaped. The doors opened. The dead began to file out, Glynn and Yarker.

She could run but she'd never outdistance them.

The dead knocked into her, attempting to carry her along with their tide. Katy's back slammed into a traffic pole. She turned and used it for purchase, fingers sliding against metal. She wrapped her left leg around the pole, pressed her cheek to it. At the front of the building, Amos flickered into view. He emerged slowly, an almost image pressed against grey stone until he sat as flesh and blood. Of course, he was one of them or something to do with them. He'd never been a man.

The last of the dead to leave the building, a woman with curly grey hair set against a youthful face, stooped and dug into Amos' box. He nodded. She removed something and headed in Katy's direction, a thin smile painted onto a taut face. The wind pulled at Katy, desperate to pull her away from the pole. If she could hold on until all the dead had passed, the world may resurge and she could go home.

It wasn't to be. The dead woman stopped at the pole, unaffected by the drag of the wind. "I'm Marcie Todd. I belong to him. You belong to him."

Marcie jabbed the sharp edge of a cocktail umbrella (no doubt what she'd removed from the box of things) into the back of Katy's hands — jab, jab, jab — forcing Katy to go.

The dead carried her away.

SEVENTEEN

Katy. Katy. Katy.

The girl's name spun cobwebs within Isobel's brain.

"Katy, don't," Isobel whispered, lips cracking open. "Katy, don't. Katy, don't die... take Peter... piss me off."

One of the above.

Her left shoulder creaked forward, fingers sweeping arcs in the dust. Her head was full of dust. Felt like sawdust. She was a fake person. She couldn't be the Isobel who wanted to marry a boy named Peter. That girl had been all twinkly, happy and annoying. Giddy. This Isobel wasn't giddy. Head too full of dust to be empty-headed.

"Katy, don't."

Who was Katy? If only she could remove the fog from her brain. Dig in past eyeballs or stuff fingers up nostrils and pull out the truth of Katy. Despite its leaden weight, Isobel's arm lifted. She traced her cheekbones. Skin smooth, not rotten. The other dead weren't rotten either. Angry grey specimens.

Her hand couldn't ball into a fist. Fingernails could scratch though. Scrape the skin off a living girl named Katy. She didn't like Katy. She didn't know why.

"Katy, don't... stand and breathe all over me."

Their breath angered Isobel. She used to breathe. Or offer a lot of hot air as her dad had said. Isobel is full of hot air and we don't understand why Peter hangs off every breath. Peter loved her. She must have loved Peter once. Or the girl she was supposed to be had loved Peter. She must be a mannequin, a false thing. She couldn't recall crawling from her grave. She remembered the worms though.

The worms ate her memories.

EIGHTEEN

The dead and Katy arrived at a residential street with a community centre on the corner (within which the dead rioted), a disused dairy on the opposite side of the street and some boarded-up shops. Although this was the living world, it currently belonged to the dead to destroy as they pleased. Her body ached. The wind had almost torn her limbs from their sockets and the dead had crushed what the wind had failed to dismember. She was a broken puppet and the dead would never let her go.

Offering the night whoops, two dead men jumped from an upper window of the community centre. Although their legs snapped beneath them, the men pulled themselves up and readjusted their bones. They cut across the street to the dairy, first at a limp and than at a run. An abandoned milk float snarled behind rusting gates.

"Someone needs to put you on a leash," Katy shouted to the milk float and the dead. Tether them to their graves.

Only one of the dead didn't participate in the riot. Marcie. Separated from the pack, Marcie stood outside a house a little way up the street. Light glowed from the hallway of the house illuminating the stained glass fanlight, whereas the other houses in the street were in darkness. Almost in shadow, as if ink had spilled from the sky to blot out the places of no interest to the dead. Katy headed towards the house.

Marcie said, "Magic lives here. The world sees an empty space. That's all we are to them. However, we're cutting into the world, making their spaces emptier, leaving gaps for others to slip in. This was our world and will be ours again."

Katy rubbed the back of her hand. The skin stung from Marcie and the cocktail umbrella's attack. Her knee ached, reminding her of its injury.

"Who lives here?" Katy asked.

She'd never known the dead to be so lucid. She should head back to the community centre and try to talk to Glynn. But, she was leaving him. Better she continue into the blacked out parts of the street, hide within the dark until the dead passed on.

"The boy who left me."

Katy understood that motivation. If this dead girl fought to reclaim her man why had Glynn forgotten her? Perhaps he'd never loved her. Katy's stomach churned. Heart ached. Actual pain stabbed between her breasts. She never wanted to believe that. Marcie knocked on the front door.

"You should go. Scoot, flee, before I tear the house down on top of you."

"I won't let you hurt someone."

"Silly little girl," Marcie said, as though she were decades older than Katy.

"If you loved him in life, if you cared for him, don't hurt him just because you're dead and he isn't."

"I'm not the one who's supposed to be dead. He is."

Along the street, glass shattered. Smoke drifted, obliterating what the ink had not. Before Katy could question Marcie, the front door opened. Opened and then tried to shut almost as fast. Marcie jammed her foot in the doorway.

"Did you miss me, Andrew?"

I'm not the one who's supposed to be dead. He is.

"Who's there?" Andrew asked, standing on tiptoes and looking over Marcie's head. "Why won't my door shut? I should call the landlord."

"Seriously," Katy said.

"Would you believe he was in an amateur dramatics club? I so wish I hadn't wasted my life going to your performances."

Andrew heard that.

"I'm going to bury you here."

"Marcie, honey... We were good together, I'll admit, but you wanted me to live again. You prayed for this, several Hail Marys and one Our Father, and there isn't a day I don't thank you for it, even though you only gave me a half-life. Actually, I'm the one who should be angry."

Andrew winked at Katy.

"I'm going to crush you."

"So he's alive and you're dead but it should be the other way around. What sort of twisted plan is that?"

"Exactly," Marcie said. "Please leave or..."

Marcie's fist flew out and the cocktail umbrella scratched down

Katy's face from beneath her eye to the corner of her lip. It gouged into skin. Katy hit out, knocking Marcie's hand aside. Blood bubbled on the end of the stick. Andrew took the opportunity to shut the door. Katy wiped her hand across her face; a streak of blood covered the back of her palm. Bitch.

"Look what you've done," Marcie said.

Marcie kicked at the garden wall. Kicked and kicked and kicked until a brick dislodged. She launched the brick at the window. Glass smashed, peppering the air before disappearing in the overgrown garden. Clearing a path through the broken window, Marcie climbed into the house. Katy knew she should hide within the dark until the dead moved on, but the idea a dead boy could live again intrigued her. Wrapping her jacket around her fist, Katy smashed the remaining shards of glass, knocking them onto the carpet, and climbed into the house. There were answers here.

The parlour walls slid in and out of ruin. One moment they offered cream flock wallpaper, the next soot-blackened walls. Katy trod between furniture and debris, the parlour landscape in constant flux. The door lurched from its hinges, swiping against the wall, gouging at plaster and burnt paper. She headed towards the sound of Andrew's voice.

"You don't love me. Love isn't this rage. On the night we crashed, I was breaking up with you. We were breaking up with each other. But oh no, you don't remember that. Weeks in the hospital distorted your view of our past. We were and we are over."

Marcie stood with her back to the kitchen doorway. The kitchen alternated between burned-out shell and 1970s appliances. A soda stream hissed on the countertop.

"Did I haunt you? No. I may have been the dead one in our non-relationship but you haunted me. You should have let me be."

Andrew looked over Marcie's shoulder to Katy. "You should let him be."

Andrew winked at Katy.

Marcie spun around. "I should kill you. Take your life and regain mine. You could be with your man all the time. You'd like that. I'd be doing you a favour."

"Didn't you hear me, Marcie? I don't want you."

"He doesn't mean it. He loves me."

"Yet he sounds so sure." Do not antagonise insane dead women. "Sorry. I wanted Glynn back. I thought you'd understand."

Behind Marcie, Andrew snorted and said, "This half-life isn't back. You think you can dig him up, stuff him back in his body and go out to tea. Four walls and remembering who you are, that's all you get. He'll still be a bloody ghost."

Marcie's shoulders sagged. She raged into the kitchen. The house began to shake. Plaster dust rained from the ceiling rose and paint peeled from blackened walls. In the kitchen, cupboards dropped to cracked linoleum. Wood blackened as unseen flames crackled up walls and across wood. Smoke billowed, seeping from the walls as if a dozen vents hid beneath wallpaper. Katy grabbed the stair rail. The house lurched forward. It seemed an impossible distance between the end of the stairs and the front door. Cobwebs draped from newel post to the wall. Katy pushed through them, tasting their silk on tongue and skin. The cut on her cheek smarted. Desperate for clean breath, Katy coughed against smoke, tried to waft it from her face. In the kitchen, Marcie and Andrew fought. The front door handle shattered within Katy's grip.

Digging her fingers into the hole left by the handle, Katy yanked at the door. Each jerk ached through her shoulder. The door fell towards her, almost knocked her over. It dropped with a crash. Katy clambered over the door, her heel cutting through rotten wood. She stumbled along the path. The weight of the house pressed against her back as if it was leaning against her, as if she were the only thing keeping it standing. Weeds tore at her ankles, desperate to tether her. Back on the pavement, Katy fell to her knees. The world was on fire. The world was falling down.

Peter emerged from the smoke. He dragged at her arm, trying to pull her into the road. Andrew's house offered the night a terrific scream, bricks and mortar fighting against each other. Katy pushed Peter off and stood. For a moment, she stared at the house and its terrific dance, swaying back and forth as though about to vomit its innards. The house collapsed in on itself burying Marcie and Andrew. Dust billowed, turning the night ash-white. The factory whistle cried, gathering its dead. They moved about her, brushing against her skin.

Within the dust, Peter cried her name. Glynn didn't.

As the wind blew the debris of the house's collapse to a neighbouring street, Marcie and Andrew clambered from the ruin. They joined the other dead, their clothes neat and grey and their skin unmarked. What they had done to the world did not touch them.

Wiping dirt from his face, Peter emerged from the dust. "We should never have found them. No one should see their dead."

"But you haven't given up on Isobel."

She'd given up on Glynn; had been prepared to leave.

"I thought I could make her remember me. Now, of course, they won't let me leave."

The dead didn't get to keep the living any more than the living could keep the dead.

"I wish I could stop loving her."

THE BUREAU OF THEM

Katy wanted to offer an Amen.

A fire engine sped around the street corner. Lights flickered on in houses along the street and people began to emerge. Where Andrew's house had stood there was now an empty plot. The dead had gone.

"They've gone on without us."

"And, I suppose that's the point," Peter said.

She couldn't argue with that.

NINETEEN

"Nobody escapes death," Yarker said.

He counted the numbers of his dead and counted again. The number was correct but their positions were not. Two of the dead sat together attempting to use the same mouse and the same screen. The correct number of dead but... Yarker shivered between the tables. Wrong. Wrong. Wrong. In the hallway, he noticed her absence. Yarker tapped on the reception desk — as though it was a coffin and he believed Isobel buried within.

He looked towards the emergency exit and the steps beyond. He'd not venture up there. He'd not ventured up there since the day he'd fallen to his death. He'd chased the only ghost he'd wanted to up those stairs. Said ghost had betrayed him and had turned out to be inhuman. Said ghost had kissed Yarker's forehead before dropping him several storeys; left his body broken amid a box of things Amos had claimed represented their connection.

The only connection here was death.

At least Yarker knew he had conquered that.

TWENTY

Katy had missed thirteen calls. She deleted the messages without listening to them, her mind fogged with other things. The Lego house remained where she'd left it on the third stair from the bottom. Peter picked up the Lego house.

"They left it for me. Some sort of warning, I think."

"I left it. Sorry. I thought it would persuade you to stay away from us, frighten you. Of course, there's no keeping us from those we love. We broke through the barriers of death. Go us."

Go them indeed.

"They're in their graves," Peter said. "We have to remember that. I don't know what they are."

"Not them," Katy said. Katy hoped.

"It's as if someone captured their image when they died and made puppets in their form."

"Puppets can't disappear."

Forget Glynn. She could chase him forever, waste away alongside him, and not win him back. Tears stung the cut on her cheek.

"He's gone," she said. She'd uttered those words a thousand times in the past thirteen months. She'd never believed them.

"We haven't escaped. As much as I'd like to think they're done with us, we don't get to walk away. Last time, Yarker dragged me back to the building. Knees, shins and elbows were raw for a week. This time," Peter said, shuddering. "Well they don't forgive the living for being able to walk away. Do you have any food? I've been living on scraps these past months."

Now he mentioned it, Katy found she was hungry and thirsty.

She hadn't thought of food or drink when she'd been with the dead. She rubbed her belly.

"We don't think about our bodys' needs and thus they take us," Peter said.

"I'll make cheese on toast." She paused in the kitchen doorway. "Who's Amos?"

"Something malevolent, I expect."

The metallic owl buzzed in her jacket pocket, vibrating against her hip. She'd forgotten it was there.

"He's not on our side, Katy."

She dug into her coat, cupped the owl. "I never thought it would hurt more to see Glynn again. That I'd rather he'd remained gone forever. Does that mean I didn't love him enough?"

She didn't need Peter to answer. Of course, it didn't mean that. In the distance, the tobacco factory blew its whistle. Faint sound carried on a determined wind. Peter paled, steadied himself against the mantelpiece, Katy's heart quickened its beat.

"We don't escape them," Peter said.

Katy pushed aside the blinds and peered at the street. The dead faded into view, marching two by two around the corner of the street. Aside from the dead and despite the hour (five o'clock), the road was unoccupied. Katy dropped the blinds, allowing them to swish back into place.

"Have you considered rescuing Isobel when the dead are occupied elsewhere? Assuming she needs rescuing."

Peter shook his head.

"If you don't try."

Shadows pressed against the window blinds. The dead amassed outside her house. They were at her door. They would destroy her house as they had destroyed those other places. It wouldn't matter that the property wasn't derelict. She'd stolen into their world. The gloves were off. The destruction of her things didn't bother Katy. It was the destruction of their things, of her memories with Glynn. He'd tear apart treasured items and not recognise a photograph or a sketch. For her, death had already taken the only thing that mattered. As Katy and Peter stole out the back door, windows shattered and the front door was ripped from its frame.

"We'll never get to the building before them," Peter said.

They needed transport. But on this side of reality, the only working vehicles were those in scrap yards or rusting on bricks outside houses and they were more interested in eating or crushing them than giving them a ride.

"Then we should start running."

It was a good three-quarter hour jog into town. By the time they reached Kensington, Katy's shins were already paining. A Hackney cab parked across two lanes, thus in the middle of the road, would not be the miracle it appeared. They approached with caution. The driver lay slumped across the steering wheel. Katy knocked on the cab window. The driver stirred and when he turned to look at them, she saw that his face was a shade of almost-grey. Taking a deep breath, Katy opened the back door and climbed in.

"The Strand."

The driver fired up the engine. He looked more embarrassed than confused at having parked across the lane and falling asleep at the wheel. As he turned the car in the right direction, Katy's right thigh pulsed, dancing against the seat. Hurry up. Peter drummed his fingers against his knee. Her house was small; it wouldn't take much to wreck. She should have at least saved her wedding dress and some photographs. She should have at least saved Glynn.

Still time for that.

"Roads sure are empty," the driver said. He removed one hand from the wheel and rubbed his chest. "Not normally like this even on a Sunday. Unless it is Sunday. You know, for the life of me, I can't remember what day it is or who I am. It keeps flitting in and out. I'm Jack and then... Do you know who I am?"

"Jack," Katy said, fingers biting into the seat.

"Yes, that's right. I think. Where did you want to go?"

"The Strand."

The lights ahead were red. Jack slammed his foot on the brakes.

"No," Peter groaned.

"Rules have changed Jack. We only stop at blue traffic lights."

"Sorry. My head is a wall of fog today. Blue, you say. By the way, do you recall my name?"

"Jack."

"Oh, I used to know a fellow named Jack."

Had this happened to Glynn? Jack looked into the mirror; appeared to be checking out his reflection rather than if there was any other traffic. Had Glynn faded until he couldn't remember himself let alone her? She didn't want to know this. She shouldn't know this until her time.

"I hope he doesn't empty before we get there," Peter said.

For a brief moment, real-life traffic echoed in the cab windows. It was as if they were in an alley nestled against their world and the alley was full of the dead. The other traffic faded, ghost images erased. The cab turned onto The Strand and when Katy instructed Jack to stop outside the building, both man and cab stopped together. His face emptied. The grey spread across his skin.

The building looked as abandoned as it should be. Peter pulled at the door. When it didn't open, he cupped his hands to the glass. "Isobel."

"We should try the fire escape."

Assuming there was an actual fire escape door. This was a fool's errand and they were the fools. She pulled at Peter's arm. Jittery now. Afraid Amos would emerge and turn malevolent and monstrous. As they reached the rear of the building, they found the fire exit door ajar and Jack slipping through the gap. Katy placed her foot between the door and the frame before it closed. This was it then, back into the monster's den. In hindsight, their escape had been an illusion.

A hand grasped her wrist. A voice whispered from within the dark of the stairwell, "Are you sure you want to enter? You may be trapped here forever."

She pushed the door fully open, threw light into the dark.

"What is it?" Peter asked. "What's up?"

Amos stood just inside the door. The world tipped and something dragged Katy into the building. The door shut, locking Peter outside. He slammed against the door, trying to gain access.

"Oops," Amos said. "I'm guessing you or the boy didn't steal my receptionist. Then you should both beware of dark corners and pissed-off brides. I'd offer you a talisman from my box but...no."

Amos vanished — like the ghost he was, Katy supposed. She opened the fire exit door and found a frustrated Peter pacing up the alley. They should leave.

"I think Isobel is missing," she said.

Peter stepped back, foot falling off the pavement. "No, she isn't."

"No, she isn't," a woman said, echoing Peter's words. "Hello, Peter. I haven't missed you."

"Is...Isobel. Izzy."

The door slammed again. Outside the building, Peter screamed. Inside, Katy stood in the dark with a dead woman's breath at her neck.

"Katy, don't," Isobel said. "Katy, don't move."

Of course, at Isobel's words, Katy moved. The world shifted again, knocking her over. A shadow loomed over her, wavering as if still mid-shift.

"Well, I did warn you," Amos said, shaking his box of things above her head. "Don't worry; I've planted her back behind the reception desk. May have to use rope though to keep her in place. Remarkable."

Katy pressed her hands to the floor and stood.

"Careful you don't fall," Amos said.

Now Katy heeded Isobel's advice and didn't move. She'd assumed she still stood beside the fire exit door but, if so, why couldn't she hear Peter? To her left, Amos flicked a lighter. Its flame cast yellow light across the contents of his box, which had dwindled to a tarnished cigarette case and two plastic blocks. In the momentary light, Katy noted the long drop a centimetre or so from her feet; a drop onto The Strand from a door formed from pushed out bricks. With the click of Amos' fingers, a street light illuminated. Amos tipped his box of things, allowing the contents to drop onto the floor.

"And your world shall tumble down."

Katy stooped and picked up the cigarette case and blocks. A whoosh of lighter fluid and the street light extinguished.

"Who are you?"

"I'm the man who could trap you in this stairwell or behind a desk. I could push you over the edge and you'd fall forever. I am the eyes, the ears, the soul, the heart. I am this place. I am its bricks, its mortar, the dirt on its windows, the shadow caught in its glass."

"You're just one of them. I bet you don't even remember who you were. You think you're a god of sorts but you're just a man."

Amos laughed. She would not fear him.

"I don't require scales to measure you or an eye glass to examine your thoughts."

Katy held out the cigarette case and blocks. "What are these?"

"Objects."

Katy threw the items down the stairs. A moment later, she felt the weight of the cigarette case and the blocks in her pocket where they clunked against the owl.

"We are all objects in the end. Hollowed out pieces on this chessboard," Amos said, and then faded against the wall.

She waited for her eyes to accustom to the dark before she descended the stairs. In the foyer, the dead streamed out into the day. She hadn't even realised they'd returned. She joined their number; following behind Isobel who did not turn or show any recognition. Peter waited for them on The Strand. Of course, he'd realised the door would open at some point. The door always opened and the dead always spilled out.

"Isobel," Peter said, but didn't move towards the dead.

Katy grabbed Isobel's wrist. She didn't have to pull the woman from the group, she moved willingly, shook Katy off and headed towards Peter. Katy's heart leapt. She searched the crowd for Glynn. Found him. She jogged to his side and grabbed his hand. Glynn turned. For a moment, she thought he recognised her (and maybe he did but she hoped not) but then he swatted her off.

"Go away," he cried.

If only she could. The tide of dead carried her along to their destination, to the tower blocks near her home and around the corner from the cinema. They sure were keen to destroy her neighbourhood. Outside The Flats, the ghost girl, toddler balanced on her hip, continued to push the shopping trolley. Its wheels offered short, sharp cries. Isobel stood over the trolley, peering in as if she saw a baby there, hand pressed to her belly. Peter held Isobel's hand. Go away, Glynn had said. Go away. Ice formed around her heart.

The dead filed into The Flats. Surely, they didn't intend to rip the block apart. They couldn't. She looked up the length of The Flats. Although she could go home, or at least attempt to, Katy followed the dead into the block and Isobel and Peter followed her. There seemed an inevitability about it all.

Although The Flats were to be demolished in a couple of months, a few residents remained while awaiting transfer to different rented accommodation. The dead didn't use the lifts. They climbed the stairs until they reached the thirteenth floor. Katy's thigh muscles ached, breath tight in her chest. A stitch tugged at her side. She leant against the window, looked at her ant-sized neighbourhood. Her house looked normal from this vantage point, not destroyed. Hope surged.

"Are you okay?" Peter asked.

Katy looked at Isobel and Peter's hands, the interweaving of their fingers. She wrapped her arms about her belly. Once upon a time... This was the moment to run (or limp) down the stairs, to go home and rebury Glynn. Once upon a tomorrow. Peter pulled a butterfly pin from his pocket. Isobel traced her fingers over it.

"Amos gave me this. I've wondered if it belonged to one of the dead or if it belonged to you," Peter said to Isobel.

She shook her head. Slow movements that dislodged dust from her bouffant. Katy pulled the owl, cigarette case and blocks from her pocket.

"The owl reminds me of Yarker. How he watches everyone. Its want of flight representing mine. If I could destroy it, melt it, then that may be the end of him. Perhaps that is Amos' plan."

Peter curled his hand around the butterfly pin and crushed it until its delicate pale-blue wings snapped. He threw its remains onto the concrete floor and slammed his heel onto it until the pin broke into several pieces. Isobel threw its remains down the stairwell.

"They all fall down," Isobel said, echoing what Amos had said to Katy in a different stairwell.

Isobel tugged Peter's hand and pulled him onto the landing. The dead swarmed into the flat. The stink of cat pee filled hall and flat. Katy held her breath. A mural decorated one wall of the flat — palm trees, blue skies and white sand — and someone had drawn their own images over it — tower blocks falling, wasteland, all in black ink; all in Glynn's hand.

TWENTY-ONE

It is impossible for me to love. Death has destroyed feeling along with body.

I want to love.

I no longer need to love.

What is love?

TWENTY-TWO

While the dead raged in other parts of the flat, Katy traced her fingers over Glynn's graffiti. Something of him remained, buried deep. The owl buzzed in her pocket, hyper, as if it and not she had discovered this truth. She wanted to point the mural out to Yarker, who stood whistling by the window admiring the view. Glynn isn't yours. A part of him exists and like Isobel, he will break through. One should always have hope, even when faced with death.

Isobel reached out, scratched her fingers down the mural and ripped a section of ink black palm tree. Peter grabbed Isobel's shoulders and pulled her to him. She smiled at him; her smile a copy of Yarker's. Glynn exited a bedroom and came to examine the destruction of his art. Isobel struggled within Peter's grip, dragging herself from him with a laugh. Free, she grabbed Glynn's hand, as if they were the lovers here, and together they began to tear the mural from the wall.

"Isobel."

Peter did not have Isobel back. Of course, he didn't. Beware of pissed-off brides. Peter slumped against the window. All fight ripped from him along with his heart. Having destroyed the mural, Isobel offered Peter her attention. She leaned in as if to kiss him but instead she placed kisses on the window behind him, a spattering of them. Then she pressed her hands to Peter's chest, offering a gentle touch; almost loving if you ignored the cracks spreading across the window, forming wings. Offering a final kiss, this time to Peter's lips, Isobel pushed her lover through the window.

Only Katy screamed.

The reverberation from Peter's fall from the thirteenth floor and his subsequent landing shivered through the flat. The dead turned to Katy. Or almost all of them did. Glynn kept his back to her. The draught from the broken window encircled her ankles, tugged at them as if desiring she follow Peter. Instead, Katy pushed through the dead and ran from the flat. The dead did not follow her.

Glynn did not follow her.

Thank god for that.

At the bottom of the stairs, the broken remains of the butterfly pin crunched beneath her shoe. Peter's ghost stood in the doorway dressed in grey suit and a tie illustrated with the rotting wings of butterflies, a permanent reminder of his folly.

"I'm sorry, Peter."

He flinched.

"Peter," she said, recalling the taxi driver had moments of lucidity at first.

He cupped his hand to his ear and squinted, as though she and her voice were distant things. She moved around him, disturbing air but not the ghost-man. A lump caught in her throat. Peter's body had landed in the ghost-girl's trolley. Blood dripped, making Spirograph patterns on concrete. She held onto her stomach. Just. She ran. ==== =When she reached the old cinema, life resurged. Traffic offering exhaust fumes, beeps of horns, people chatting; normality.

"Katy."

Not Katy-Kate. It didn't sound like Glynn's voice.

"For god's sake, Katy, slow down."

Nathan pressed his hand to his chest and caught his breath. Katy stared at him, seemed to have left her voice amongst the dead. "I've been trying to contact you for days. So has Steph. We've phoned, called round. Where've you been?"

"I... a friend wasn't well. He died."

"Who?"

"No one you know."

A scream cut across the street. Nathan turned towards The Flats. Someone had found Peter's corpse. In her pocket, the owl danced against her thigh. Considering what had happened to Peter after destroying the butterfly pin, she should keep it safe. She wanted to throw it though and forget everything that happened.

"Nathan to Katy," Nathan said, snapping his fingers.

"Sorry."

"Thought I'd lost you there."

Nathan always built his words so well.

"So you're coming to the pub?"

"What time?"

"Five minutes ago. It's after five."

"Of course it is. I'm just running behind."

Across the street, the metal shutter fell from the cinema doorway. A car swerved to avoid it. It would be safer for her to spend time with the living.

"Let's go," Katy said, linking arms with Nathan.

The Old School stood at the corner of Boaler Street and Sheil Road and across from The Flats. A fire engine chased by an ambulance sped around the corner, blue lights whirring in competition. A crowd had gathered around the shopping trolley, around Peter's corpse. Katy could no longer see the ghost-girl, her toddler or Peter's ghost. Her fingers dug into Nathan's arm.

"It's good to have you back. Hey," Nathan said, grabbing her wrist. "What's this?"

"Just some stamp from a nightclub. I need to wash it off."

"Is that the name of the club?"

"Can't remember. Must be. If you could see Glynn again, just for a moment, what would you say to him?"

Better things than she had said, she hoped.

"I don't know. Maybe if he wanted a pint. Yes, I'd like to have a pint with him one more time. Pretend it was old times. Of course, we'll never see him again so..."

"It was just a question. So who else will be here?"

"Steph and Dan. You don't mind Dan being there... here?"

Steph waved from a booth by the window.

"Makes no difference to me. Hardly a revolution though. Can four people save a pub? I suspect it'll still be torn down as the whole area is in flux."

There were reasons people had stopped drinking here, namely the rotting décor and the temperament of the manager. Daniel stood to let Katy into the booth.

"Right then," Nathan said, rubbing his hands together. "What's everyone having?"

When everyone had given their orders, Steph jumped up. "I'll help Nathan with the drinks." She winked at Daniel.

Suddenly, Katy would rather spend time with the dead.

"I think this is the first time we've been alone."

Shit.

"I've been meaning to..."

She stood, a little too fast and a little too hard — her knee cracked against the table.

"Are you okay?"

"I need the loo."

"Oh, of course," Daniel said, stepping from the booth.

The pub doors crashed open, slamming into beer-stained pillars at either side, and although the building shook, quaked within its foundations, only Katy noted the storm. The dead were here.

TWENTY-THREE

The living did not see the dead. Those who were his friends did not see Glynn. She should have thrown away the owl and risked the consequences. The dead swaggered and danced between the tables. Still the living took no note of them. Nathan and Steph carried four drinks between them. Marcie's elbow jostled Nathan's arm causing him to drop a glass. Whiskey sloshed over his shoes. Nathan looked about him, as if he'd felt Marcie's knock, but there was no one (visible) close to him.

"They're here," Katy said.

"About time."

"Some fucker knocked a drink out my hand."

"I saw," Katy said.

"See I told you, it wasn't my clumsiness."

Behind them, Yarker climbed onto the bar. "Attention, breath bags. You're all going to get smashed into bite-sized pieces because she let us in. Take a bow, miss."

"What?" Katy asked.

"Katy, sit down," Steph said.

"Can't you hear him? Can't you see them?"

Of course they couldn't. The show was for her. Glynn moved behind the bar, performing a dance with the bartender who remained oblivious. Steph leaned across the table and pulled at Katy's jacket. The metallic owl and cigarette case fell out, both items proving phantoms to the living. Marcie snatched the cigarette case. She danced away with it. Marcie who was now fully dead after a house had fallen on her head. There was no sign of ghost-Peter.

"Keep it. I don't want it."

"Katy, who the fuck are you talking to?" Nathan asked.

"I know you can't see them. I know you think I'm mad." She made a half-strangled noise as pain stabbed her chest. "The dead are here, Glynn is here, and I think they intend to hurt us."

"Glynn isn't here," Nathan said, but he rubbed his elbow and considered the room.

"I should leave," Katy said.

They all should.

Steph said, "You're not going anywhere. We're going to talk about this until we've made you understand Glynn is dead."

"Don't patronise me. I never said he wasn't. Something is happening here. Heck, you don't even have to believe me, just trust we should leave. Is that so big a thing to ask?"

Isobel and two other dead encircled Katy. Glass smashed on the other side of the pub. The air stunk of liquor. Further glass smashed. A crescendo of destruction as bottles rained from the bar. People stood to check the chaos but no one fled and no one screamed. Katy's wrist burned, her fingers tore at the company stamp. Marcie pushed through the dead trio. She popped open the cigarette case allowing the hand-rolled cigarettes to drop to the floor. She kept the match. Marcie rested its combustible tip to the strike on the back of the case. All that liquor. All that ale. Katy awaited the whoosh. She could hardly breathe for the expectation of it.

"We have to get out. Everyone needs to get out. Now."

No one turned or appeared to hear her words. She'd drifted into the alley between life and death. The match flared. A man at the next table pointed at the glow, as if that one thing transferred between worlds.

"You were like them once," Katy said. She turned to her friends. "I need you to trust me. Heck, you can have me sectioned after this if you want, but please leave the pub right now. Whatever happens please don't hesitate. Humour me."

Nathan and Daniel stood. However, Steph remained seated, arms folded.

"Bloody hell Steph, I lost my man not my mind." Katy grabbed Steph's arm and pulled her from the booth. The match tasted liquor. The air whooshed. Now people screamed. Now they moved. With his good-old-perfect timing, Glynn finally looked at her, recognised her, and winked that old wink of his. If she didn't leave know she'd never escape, but now that he looked at her she couldn't run. Now Steph pulled at her arm until the crowd parted them and carried Steph, Nathan and Daniel from the pub. At the back of the pub, Yarker sat on a man, rode him as if he were a horse, pinning him in place. Glynn jumped from the bar into the melee.

"This isn't you."

He stopped in front of her. Chin to her forehead, looked down at her. His hands traced her wrists. Her fingers trembled. She'd waited so long to hold his hands again. Instead, his fingers traced her hips and then dipped into her pocket. He removed the blocks.

"And they all fall down."

Glynn dropped the blocks and crushed them beneath his shoe. Above them, the ceiling shifted.

"I loved you."

The pub windows shattered. Glynn grabbed her, twirled her around to shield her from the stab of glass. He hoped to save her. Instead, his act killed her. Katy's knees gave out first. Breath caught in her throat and refused to return. Glynn's arm remained around her. He'd come back to her. She had to believe that. Fire roared but it didn't matter now. What mattered, what would kill her, was the glass shard that cut into her heart.

"I don't want to..." she said, but then her head clouded and her first word on waking in a poorer, greyer world was "...die."

The ceiling fell, crushing her body and shielding it from her ghost eyes. Flames danced but she couldn't feel their heat. Ash rained, leaving her skin greyer. There was sorrow in Glynn's eyes. There was sorrow in all their eyes. This time, they followed her from the building as if she pulled their strings.

The world had changed. Where The Flats had stood there was now only dust and rubble. New dead walked amongst the ruin. Yarker gathered his old dead to him, leaving Katy alone. She didn't belong with them. Her place wasn't in an old building on The Strand, her death had seen to that. She was this old pub and The Flats. Emergency vehicles haunted the edges of the scene but they were nothing to her. The recent dead moved through the rubble, picking their way to her. They awaited her instruction. They needed somewhere to play with the rage that bubbled in their bellies. Their rage was her rage. They were as one. They were as her.

Katy walked by her dead (they followed her) and found Peter standing on a hillock of rubble alongside the ghost girl and her toddler. She'd lost a baby. It lived in the world, breathed and laughed and joked and played; left her behind. This made the ghost girl angry. It made Katy angry too. How dare the ghost-girl's daughter live on in the world when her mother was gone. She should have died with grief. They should all die with grief. She'd wanted to die once, when the man she loved had died. Steph, Nathan and Daniel gathered about the broken jukebox. They danced on the records, smashing them, adding to the destruction. Katy called them to her. They turned and followed in a way they'd never have done so in life. They would make their home in the cinema. Settle in its rafters. From the roof, they would survey the streets for empty places, places where the dead fought against walls and windows. They would free them. They would free all ghosts.

From the rubble, Katy picked up a troll-like doll with a shock of green hair, a broken wristwatch, a strip of photo-booth pictures, a fountain pen, a dirt-brown teddy bear — things to keep the living occupied until they joined their numbers, until they became them. Amos waited at the cinema doors. She placed almost all her things in his box, knew he could haunt here and The Strand.

"I have no living," she said, "but they do. Bring them to us."

The one item she kept — the fountain pen. She would use it to ink 'The Bureau of Them, Us and You' on the skin of her dead.

SNOWBOOKS HORROR NOVELLAS

ALBION FAY

Mark Morris

Albion Fay, a holiday house in the middle of nowhere, surrounded by nature's bounty. For the adults, a time for relaxation and to recharge the batteries, while for the children, a chance for exploration and adventure in the English countryside. A happy time for all: nothing could possibly go wrong. Or could it? What should be a magical time ends in tragedy – but what really happened that summer?

SCOURGE

Gary Fry

Felachnids: a race of mythical creatures that are rumoured to live in the dark Yorkshire countryside.

The yellow eyes, the double-jointed limbs, the heads that turned backwards whenever that was necessary. These creatures, which otherwise resembled humans, appeared to occupy a small village in North Yorkshire called Nathen.

And Lee Parker is determined to track them down.

SNOWBOOKS HORROR NOVELLAS

THE NINE DEATHS OF DR VALENTINE

John L. Probert

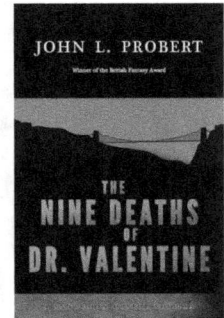

Someone is killing doctors in the style of the murders in Vincent Price movies, leaving the Bristol police baffled. The only man who could possibly be responsible died years ago... or did he... ?

The police in Bristol have been confronted by a series of the most perplexingly elaborate deaths they've ever encountered in all their years of murder enquiries. The only thing which connects them is their seemingly random nature and their sheer outrageousness. As Detective Inspector Longdon and his assistant Sergeant Jenny Newham (with the help of pathologist Dr. Richard Patterson) race against time to find the murderer, they eventually realise that the link which connects the killings is even more bizarre than any of them dared to think....

www.snowbooks.com